I0548751

Taking Wainui

Laura Solomon

Published by Woven Words Publishers OPC Pvt. Ltd.,
2017

ISBN-13: 978-81-934093-5-0
ISBN-10: 8193409353
Price: $ 15

Woven Words Publishers OPC Pvt. Ltd.,
Vill: Raipur, P.O: Raipur Paschimbar, Dist: Purba
Midnapore, Pin: 721401, West Bengal, India.
www.wovenwordspublishers.net

Acknowledgements:

Many of the stories in this collection have been previously published.

Taking Wainui, The Fiction Pool, UK, 2017

The Scar, Punch Magazine, India, 2017, TBC

Subterranean Ghost Station Blues, LE Poetry and Writing, Bali Indonesia, 2017.

The New Valve, Aphelion, United States, 2017

White Lotus, Blackmail Press, NZ, East of the Web, United States, 2017

The Sammy Series, Short Humour Site, UK, 2017

Fresh Wolves, The Moth, Ireland, 2012

The Rising Epidemic of Bullying, Maple Tree Literary Supplement, 2012, Landfall essay competition, runner up 2012.

Dying Matters, Takahe, 2012, NZ

The Transcripts of Venus, Headstuff, UK, 2013?

The Long Walk Home, Authors Electric Guest Post, 2012, UK.

Contents

TAKING WAINUI

They made me drink piss out of a gumboot. Not just a sip but half a litre or so. Disgusting. I was sick everywhere afterwards, no surprise really. Then they told me that was just the beginning. O the joys of being a Prince Mamba leader's son. People said I was doomed to end up in the gangs – born to it. What a life, what a curse.

My childhood was not a normal one, but of course I only know that now. We lived in a rented state house in Kaiti, with three wrecked Holdens parked abandoned in the drive. A couple of pit bulls kept guard. There were always gang members loitering around the house, chucking their empty beer cans wherever it suited them. I used to try and clean up but I was fighting a losing battle. My two older brothers were initiated at eighteen and they became just like Dad – ruling with iron fists. Mum was dominated by Dad, who ruled over everybody. He would have tyrannized the whole town, the whole of New Zealand, if he'd had his way. My Mum was spaced out on Valium a lot of the time. Dad would have killed her if she'd tried to leave. No family member taught me the practicalities of life – I learnt how to cross roads at school. No adult ever read me a bedtime story.

It was my Uncle Taika who taught me how to surf. Surfing saved my life. Whenever I got sad or angry I would just take the board my uncle bought me and head out to the waves. I had to keep the board at my uncle's house or Dad and his mates would have just sold it for drug money. I used to dream of being Australasian surf champion. It was in the waves that I met my first and only real friend Kya. Kya was tall for her age and thin and she was a demon on the board. I wasn't in love with her or anything corny like that but she was a good friend; somebody I could really talk to about all the many problems at home. She didn't judge me on my background which was more than you could say for most of the herd in my classroom. We just enjoyed each other's company. It was good to feel accepted by *somebody* on planet Earth.

I had been dreading my initiation ceremony. There was no question that I would join the gangs, because of who my father was. It wasn't my own wish at all – it was just something that you did in my family – kind of like some kids growing up with everyone assuming they will go to university. My Dad would have beaten me to a pulp if I ever thought about not joining. My life circumstances made it very tough for me to assert myself. Earlier in the year at school there had been a program run by the police on stopping youth from getting into gangs and a Pakeha lady called Jasmine had come to our school to talk to us about it. Was it just my imagination or had she had taken a special shine to me? When she spoke it seemed as if she was talking directly to me and I wondered whether she knew I was a Prince Mamba leader's son. At the end of the week she took me to one side and asked me what my ambitions in life were. I told her I wanted to be a pro surfer and didn't mention that it was a lot more likely that I would end up being a fully patched gang member. She smiled and nodded when I talked about surfing and commented that Gisborne had some gnarly waves. I couldn't believe she had used the word gnarly, like a teenager. Perhaps she was trying to be down with the kids.

When the big day rolled around, my eldest brother took me to one side and told me that it was time for me to be a man. I had witnessed other initiation ceremonies and did not see how drinking urine from a gumboot was a mark of manhood but I didn't say anything. I drank as much of the piss as I could and then was sick everywhere. Then Dad's right hand man Rangi, took me to one side and told me I was going to have to do a burglary. Rangi has 'We ride together, we die together' tattooed across his neck. He said he was letting me off lightly and that there didn't have to be violence or firearms involved. Sometimes there can be rape or even murder in the initiations, or taking the rap for somebody else's crime and doing hard time in their place. They told me that they had chosen a do-gooder target in posh Wainui Beach so that there would be lots of loot. Wainui Beach residents are all loaded.

Rangi said that Jimmy would drive me to the job. He said he could take one of the better cars for it, so that all those nice white middle class residents would not be alerted to our purpose. The deal was to go down on Saturday night when a lot of people would be out partying, leaving their houses empty and ripe for the picking.

When Saturday rolled around I was dead nervous. What if the cops caught me? I was only seventeen and I didn't want to end up in prison. My Dad had been put away numerous times; we'd just had to soldier on without him. He said that clink was softer than his life on the outside, he reckoned prison made him into a pussy. He didn't have to fend for himself in there, you see, he was provided for by the government. He had friends on the inside and they all stuck together, in a gang, just like on the outside. My father was King Dick in prison. I couldn't imagine being inside; in a small, cold cell. Three solid meals a day mind you, and a guaranteed place to sleep at night, rent-free, maybe it wouldn't be all bad.

We waited till 11pm and then drove the car slowly through Wainui Beach. I thought we looked terribly suspicious and kept telling Jimmy to speed up a bit, to drive authoritatively, so that it looked as if we knew where we were going. I got out at the start of Wairere Road and started walking through people's back sections trying to find a house that looked deserted. It was hard to tell because most people had all their lights out. At number 35 I stumbled across somebody's dog, a huntaway, that started barking loudly at me.
Oh God, I thought, *just what I need to alert the neighbours for miles around.*
Eluding the vocal dog as quickly as I could I darted around the side of what appeared to be a wood shed, I waited for about a minute until the dog became bored and started sniffing under a hedge for the elusive hedgehog he'd been after for months. Adrenaline was coursing through me - I'd never been so petrified in my life; I just wanted this over with.

Thankfully the next house appeared deserted - no car, no lights on and most importantly no dogs.
I skulked up the outside stairs to the back door where I found a cat flap. I had done this once before when I had gone around to my uncle's house unexpectedly and he hadn't been home. After shivering on the doorstep for half an hour I had reached up through the cat door and managed to turn the key in the lock. My lankiness I had often been teased about came in handy in this instance.

Reaching through the cat door I discovered it was a lock with a push button in the handle - this was unnervingly easy. I was in! Heading straight for the bedroom, unzipping my bag as I walked, I found an Ipad on the duchess that became my first stolen item. Opening the drawers next, I found a phone, some jewellery and a wallet. I put it all in my bag. I hesitated, thinking that I could hear a noise downstairs. Listening intently I heard two car doors close.rubbing against my leg as if it had known me forever.I had to get out of here. There were sounds outside. I scanned the room looking for a window, found it, ran over to it – then remembered I was on the second floor. The sounds were inside now. I couldn't think straight so I dropped to the floor in between the bed and the wall.

I heard footsteps coming up the stairs and began to freak out even more. Although I was a gang member's son I was no hardened criminal, I only wanted to spend my life surfing. I had seen what gang life had done to my father and my brothers and I did not want to end up like them. Footsteps up the hallway now, I felt like a stoat in a trap. The door opened and I saw two long shadows cast upon the far wall. A man spoke.

"Hey, why is the top drawer of my duchess open?"

At that moment my body took over my mind and I stood up and tried to make a run for it. The man, who was solid and looked like a rugby player blocked my path. There was a brief scuffle, then he grabbed me in a headlock.

"Jasmine call the cops. We've got ourselves a thief!"

"Hang on a minute Nick. I think I know this guy."

At that moment our eyes met and I recognized her. It was the lady who had come to my school and taken a special interest in helping me stay out of the gangs. I felt so ashamed. Why did I have to target her house? The gods had it in for me. I groaned and sank to the floor despondent.

"I didn't get away with anything" I said. "Just take back what's in the backpack and let me go. This was meant to be my initiation into the gang. I didn't even want to do it but I had to. They made me."

Jasmine gave me a long look then said "Come into the lounge, I'll make you a cup of tea."

Nick grabbed the backpack from where it lay on the floor and checked its contents.

I followed Jasmine through into the lounge. She boiled the kettle and made us both a cuppa. I put three spoons of sugar in mine - I was in need of a pick me up. Then I remembered Jimmy who was driving the car. He would be wondering where I was by now. What should I do? I decided to forget about Jimmy and concentrate on Jasmine. If anybody could help me get away from gang life it was her.

"So tell me about tonight," she said. How did you come to be burgling my house?"

"I was told to by my father's right hand man. I was told that it was time for me to join the gang and that I had to take part in initiation."

"Is this the life you want?"

"No, definitely not. I can't stand violence and drugs. I'm into surfing. I don't want to end up like my father."

I breathed a heavy sigh.

"I can help you break the cycle", said Jasmine. "But you have to listen to what I say. I think you should stand up to your father and tell him that you don't want to join the gang."

I was silent. She obviously didn't know my father. We talked on for half an hour and I began to think that I had found somebody other than Kya who cared about me. It can be hard, letting your guard down and trusting somebody, even a little bit, when all you have known is cold, unkind treatment. Jasmine gave me a ride home. We talked in the car further. I knew what I had to do.

#   #   #

When I walked in through the front door I found my father pacing the living room as my mother nervously busied herself in the kitchen.
"Where the hell have you been!?" bellowed my father. "And where's the bloody loot!? Jimmy came by here an hour ago. Who gave you a lift home?"
I remembered Jasmine's words. Stand up. Stand tall, like a man.
"Look Dad, I don't want to be in the gang. I want a normal life, like a normal person. I'm not into the kind of life you lead."
My father's right fist hit my jaw with a thunderous crack. "Don't you get cocky with me, boy! Bloody mamma's boy! You're nothing but a sissy. It's time you were toughened up."
He punched me hard in the stomach and I fell to the floor. My mother was crying and screaming for him to stop but he didn't. The beating went on for what seemed like eternity and only stopped because my uncle came in and pulled my father off me when I was on the verge of unconsciousness. I could not see out of my right eye, but I went to my bedroom, gathered up my meagre belongings and put them in a backpack. I was out of there, no looking back. My father was a dangerous criminal. I couldn't stick around.

I managed to sleep a few hours and in the morning pretended I was going to school. Instead of attending I went to Jasmine's office and told her what had happened. She was horrified and said that I should move to another town and that she could get me police protection. When I asked where I should go to she suggested Nelson. She said she could provide me with the money for a plane ticket and some cash to help me find my first flat then get me hooked up with work and income. After that I said I would look for a job, maybe some bar work. She said I should stay with her for a few nights and that she would take care of me. Nobody had ever taken care of me before and I was a bit suspicious but what choice did I have? I couldn't go back to Dad's place or he would've murdered me.

Nick didn't take too kindly to having me around, but he tolerated me, since I was part of Jasmine's job. I looked online on TradeMe for places to live and made a list of four flats to visit when I was down there. Jasmine said I was doing great considering all I had been through. At night I suffered terrible nightmares about being hunted down and castrated by my father and would awake in a sweat.

A few days later I found myself on a one way flight to Nelson. I'd never been there before.
hen I disembarked from the plane, the first thing I saw was a lone yellow balloon on a string which was floating high into the sky. For some strange reason I felt a sense of serenity as if this balloon was a sign of hope and freedom. I stayed in a backpackers that first night. I barely slept and got up early to search for a place to live and a job.
Finding a flat was easy the first place I went to I moved in, I was living with three others, Jackie who was a florist, Steve who was at polytech studying personal training, and Anna who was a truck driver Finding a job didn't take long either I got a job as a barman it was tiring working late nights but the staff were great, the pay was above

average, and it was a very sociable job. It was great meeting lots of new people.

Kya was texting me flat out worried about where I was and if I was ok. She had heard from my brothers that I had received a beating from my father and that I had taken off. I didn't tell Kya where I was for her own safety's sake but I told her I would keep in touch. Apart from her and Jasmine no one was bothering to contact me which suited me fine. I wanted to forget my old life, start fresh. My flatmates and I were becoming great mates. Steve and I went to the gym together. Working out was great for my mental health. Things were going great and after two months of living in Nelson I felt myself finally relaxing. Little did I know my father hadn't finished with me yet. In a case of 'revenge is best served cold' he blindsided me.

\#   \#   \#

It was a typical Friday night at the bar where I worked. Not as busy as a Saturday night but busy enough. I was pouring a round of shots for a group of girls when out of the corner of my eye I noticed Pete and Clive the bouncers outside attempting to keep some guys from entering I walked over to the door getting ready to help. The next thing I knew the door swung violently open and two burly tattooed guys came barging in scanning the room aggressively. It took me a mere three seconds to recognize them; two of my father's plebs. What the hell were they doing here? Before I had another thought they spotted me and started to walk over. I had to think quickly. I ran for the back of the bar into the men's rooms. Locking a cubicle door behind me, I opened the small window above the loo and squeezed myself out of the small gap. Hitting the ground at a run I sprinted home hoping like hell they didn't know where I lived.

I was safe. They had tracked me down at the bar but it appeared they did not know my home address for they did not come for me there. At home I locked all the doors. Thankfully no one else was home. Anna was away working driving her truck to Queenstown, Steve was probably at the gym as he seemed to practically live there, and Jackie was no doubt at her sick grandma's where she seemed to hang out most weekends.

I located my cell phone and didn't even notice my hands were trembling until I tried to dial Jasmine's number. It was late - 12:45am. Jasmine answered after five rings with a sleepy voice.

"Tane, are you OK?

" No, they came for me Jasmine, they came for me at the bar!"

I was freaking out

"Calm down, take a deep breath. Who came for you?"

"Some of the gang. My father must have sent them to find me. I just ran, I saw it in their eyes Jasmine - they wanted blood."

There was a pause.

"Hang on a minute Tane. I'll just go talk into the lounge."

I waited.

"Right. This is what you need to do." Jasmine's authoritative tone came down the line. "It's obviously not safe for you in this country; it sounds like your father will never stop hunting you. Give me your bank account number - I'll put enough money in for you to get an emergency passport and a ticket to Australia. Go to the nearest travel agency tomorrow they will help you with both of those things."

"Ok," I said, "Thank you so much Jasmine, you've really helped me so much."

"No worries Tane I just want you to be safe, keep in touch."

Five days later I had obtained an emergency passport and a plane ticket to Sydney. My boss understood why I had to leave. My flatmates were sad to see me go and made me a nice farewell dinner the night before my flight.

Australia was great - the weather, the surfing, lots of jobs - I got a job and a flat in Manly at a bar. I finally felt safe. I didn't think the gang would bother to track me down over here.

Kya was texting and calling me a lot. I told her all about how great Australia was and all the surf spots there were and that I'd pay for her to come over to visit.

She joined me two weeks later. We became boyfriend and girlfriend not long after and were married the following spring. Children followed and much joy was brought to my life. I had been praying to god to bring me through the storm and it appeared that he had answered my prayers and I now felt safe and happy. Sometimes trials are sent to test our faith and we should lean on god to see us through. The gang members did not bother me or try to follow me to Australia and the remainder of my days on earth were blessed and happy, full of the joys of life, for I knew what it was to suffer and so I more fully appreciated the good times, the high points and felt that I was now strong enough to make it through whatever trial or tribulation life should send my way.

THE SCAR

I was dumped on a Thursday. Things hadn't been going well between us and I should've known the end was nigh. All the signs were there. The way she breathed a heavy sigh each time I entered the room. The way she rolled her eyes whenever I opened my mouth to speak. I had been diagnosed with brain cancer the previous spring. I'd undergone a craniotomy and had fallen into a slump of depression and had no doubt turned into a pain in the arse, moping around the flat and feeling sorry for myself, googling the prognosis of brain tumours and worrying incessantly about the statistics. There was a six inch scar running from one side of my head to the other. The doctor had sectioned me after my craniotomy and I had tried to run away from the psychiatric hospital and subsequently been locked in seclusion. Since then I had suffered constant nightmares about being buried alive.

My girlfriend Zoe was an interior decorator. Some people thought she was a snob. I had worked in IT for ten years until the tumour had grown in my brain, making it impossible for me to continue my work. Fortunately I'd had income protection insurance, so I wasn't dependent on my girlfriend for money – that would have been too hard for both of us to accept. We had met at a party in Ponsonby three years previously. She said that I made her laugh which not many people had the ability to do. I was on good money when we first met and sometimes I wondered if that was the main thing she liked about me.   I shouted her new clothes, dinners and vacations to L.A. and Tahiti. We got along reasonably well but only when we were both busy working. When I lost my job it was a different story.

"God why are you always just hanging around the house?", she would say. "You're such a sad sap. Can't you get out more. Be proactive. I know you've got cancer but that's no need to sit around feeling sorry for yourself. Get out and get some exercise."

She would throw a pair of jogging shoes at me.

"Look at how much weight you've put on. Can you even see your toes?"

I got the distinct feeling she wasn't attracted to me anymore, which only added to my feelings of inadequacy. My friends had also begun to drop away – I guess I talked about the tumour too much and people got sick of hearing about it.

One night there was a program on TV about people who lived within the Disability Support Service in community homes. A week later I came home from a walk to find a man and a lady in casual dress sitting on the couch drinking out of our best coffee cups. A plate of biscuits was placed on the coffee table next to a stack of Zoe's magazines.

"Hi darling. This is Liz Jacobs and Karen Islington from Disability Support Services. They're here to discuss life options with you."

"Life options! What the hell do you mean by that?"

"Wouldn't it be better if you lived with people like you. These two have a nice community home that you can go and live at. It's in Weka Street. Near a park. You could go for walks. They have a three-legged cat called Tripod."

One of the DSS workers chimed in.

"Your flatmates will be Johnny and Kate. They have disabilities too. You'll fit right in."

"I don't have a disability. I've had a brain tumour removed and I'm suffering subsequent mild depression that's all."

Zoe and the DSS workers looked at each other.

"Oh well it's all arranged. I've packed your suitcase."

She disappeared into the next room and came back with the packed case.

"I've made an appointment with the lawyer on Monday so you can talk through those contracts for that work you were thinking of doing, for the firm in town."

I didn't know what to say. I was in a state of shock. I felt like I was outside my body watching events unfold. My body grabbed the suitcase and headed for the door. I was dumped and evicted on the same day.

I was sitting at the house with Tripod on my knee. Johnny and Kate had turned out to be non verbal. They mostly just watched DVDs and sometimes were taken for walks. I settled in as best I could but it was hard to feel at home. There were staff on during the day and staff who stayed overnight doing 'sleepovers'.

On Monday, I met Zoe at the lawyer's office. She presented me with two legal forms, which were Power of Attorney documents. She tried to sweet talk me into signing them.

"I will take care of you", she promised. "Pay your bills. You won't have to worry about anything financial. It will be a weight off your shoulders. After all you've been through."

I got a bad feeling. She did not seem genuine. I did not want her taking all my money. I felt that she was trying to trick me, to swindle me. My gut instinct was telling me not to sign so I didn't. She had a small hissy fit because I had not done what she wanted me to do. I told her to get out of my life and that I did not want to see her anymore.

A DSS disco was held the following Wednesday. I attended and that's where I met Mary. Mary had had a stroke and was in a wheelchair. She had big blue eyes and a crop of thick ginger hair, but what I really liked about her was her warmth and depth. Zoe had proven herself to

21

be shallow, just out for what she could get. I had been burned by her. Mary was different. We clicked immediately, and sat talking side by side for the duration of the disco which was not really my cup of tea with its Abba music and its flashing coloured lights. Mary and I decided to catch up for a coffee the following week. She said she would pick me up because she had to get a wheelchair taxi. We met for coffee at a café at the botanical gardens. Afterwards we went for a walk. I pushed Mary in her wheelchair, getting fit as I did so.

Mary said she would take me to her favourite place – the school hall of her old primary school. We stood outside the hall where you could hear the piano playing though there was nobody in the room. A ghost? I looked through the window but I could see nobody seated at the piano although it looked as though the piano keys were being pushed down. I told Mary this but she did not believe me, so I picked her up and lifted her up to the window for her to see for herself.

We were a little freaked out so we left immediately and talking about it on the way home we decided to call in at the library to research the school's history. Searching through the library archives we discovered that twenty years ago a music teacher by the name of Mr Batt, who had been a talented piano player, had died in a tragic boating accident. He had been trapped in the hull of his boat when it capsized. Mary and I were intrigued by this and we decided to research more apparently haunted buildings. Mary had attended this primary school for seven years and she could remember Mr Batt being cruelly teased by being called Mr Fat. She said that she felt sorry for him and that she was fairly sure it was his restless spirit now playing the piano. She said that we should try to contact him. We purchased a Ouija board online and took it into the school hall, breaking in late at night. We had candles and food, just in case his ghost was hungry. We set up the board ready to start. We had written a small list of questions – the first being *Why are you not at peace?* The answer came back *The children must pay for their transgressions.* We asked another question. *Can you forgive the children?* There was a hesitation and then he answered back *Never.* There came a few angry chords on the piano. *We are your friends. We would like you to be at peace.* The grumpy reply came back. *I'll think about it - please leave now.*

Mary and I walked back through the night, thinking about what we had just experienced, and how we could help Mr Batt. We were really excited about our new found hobby – communicating with the Ouija board. As we walked Mary expressed how she wanted to help Mr Batt find peace and forgiveness. Although she was never involved in the teasing, she had witnessed it and felt a twinge of guilt. She was so kind and caring I wanted to help her achieve her goals.

"The problem is that his spirit hasn't passed over properly", said Mary. "We need to help him."

I read about Zoe's car crash in the papers. She'd been drinking and had run head first into a lorry on State Highway 12. She'd been killed instantly – thank God for small mercies. Better that than living on as a cripple. I was magnanimous. I did not harbor resentment and give in to thoughts such as *serves her right after the way she treated me* and *what goes around comes around.* I did not think *So, she has been served her just desserts.*

We contacted Mr Batt's spirit again one week later in the primary school hall. Mary summoned him using the Ouija board. She said she would help him cross over into the light. After the spirit had made its presence felt by rapping out a 'yes' in answer to the question 'Are you Mr Batt?' Mary tried to talk sense to the restless ghost.

'You need to move towards the light', she told it. 'You no longer belong on Planet Earth.'

There was a lengthy pause.

"Mr Batt, you have died and it is time for you to move on from this realm. There are people waiting for you who love you. We believe you can make it into heaven. Do not haunt this place any longer."

Some more harmonious chords were played upon the piano.

'Perhaps we have soothed his spirit", said Mary.

Nothing spectacular happened. No beam of bright white light ascended into the heavens. However, Mary and I both felt a more peaceful feeling settle over the hall as a hungry ghost was laid to rest. All was quiet and still and Mr Batt's ghost haunted the hall no more.

SUBTERRANEAN GHOST STATION BLUES

I'm from a family that some people might call privileged. My father's the CEO of some old corporation or other and my mother's a socialite that does a lot of charity work. They own the mandatory Manhattan apartment. They're *busy*, always *busy* – busy attending some corporate event or *Women Who Care Luncheon* or Violet Ball. Mother's latest project was helping out at the Coalition for the Homeless. She brought home their annual report, which stated that in New York there were currently more than 36,000 homeless people, including 15,500 children, sleeping each night in municipal shelters, while thousands more slept rough on city streets, in public parks, in the subway system and in other public spaces. That immediately made me feel a little less sorry for myself. Mum and Dad are often too busy to help me with my homework or kick a ball around in the back yard. I'm not a moper, like Dad's sister Maude. She's an artist manqué – a frustrated artist. She graduated from the School of Visual Arts in 1990, but then fell into a trough of sloth and despondency from which she never emerged. Instead of producing, she took to drinking daytime G&Ts and watching the telly. She had just one exhibition, which bombed. She developed epilepsy. If she got tired, hungry or stressed she could throw a fit.
Beware of failed artists, said my father. *They can turn nasty. Look at Hitler.* He followed this up with, *Saddam Hussein was discovered in a hole in the earth writing novels and poems of which he was the hero,* as if to suggest some intrinsic link between art and political psychopaths.

It was shortly after my thirteenth birthday that I got the idea of running away. I guess a lot of kids get a similar idea around that age, but they don't have a *plan* like I had a plan. They didn't *prepare* like I prepared. I packed my bags – clothes, toothbrush, deodorant, a map of the subway. I packed a blow-up single mattress that my parents had bought for a camping holiday in the Catskills. I had seen a programme on the telly about mole people living in the sewers underneath New York. They emerged during the day to raid the garbage cans outside posh supermarkets. They lived on this fare along with sewer rats that they roasted whole over open fires. I thought that I could have a good life with these people. It would be something different anyway. My old life was suffocating. My friends were all spoilt little rich brats with too many toys and too much spare time on their hands.

I disappeared down a manhole on the corner of 111th and 5th Streets. I guess you could say it was a vanishing of sorts. I headed into a subterranean world. The walls were black, made of dirt and damp to the touch. There was a musky smell in the air. A lighter burned up ahead of me. I headed towards its glow. In its dull light, I could see that the walls of the subway had been decorated by graffiti artists; taggers. Two or three mole people began moving towards me. They moved so softly that it seemed they had webbed feet. They made strange noises that seemed barely human, but that was their way of communicating with one another.

They drew closer. One at a time they introduced themselves to me. None of them used their real names. They used invented names instead; Scar, Hammer, D-dog. Their clothes were ripped and tattered and they stank to high heaven.

There are about six thousand of us, said Scar. *Us underground people. Us mole people. Some of us have been down here for over a decade.*

They told me various facts or fictions about their past lives. Above ground they had been prostitutes or strippers or worked at checkouts. One guy claimed to have been a lawyer. Drug addiction was rife down here. Most of these sewer dwellers shot up or smoked crack or both. They had to, in order to dull the pain of their daily lives. An atmosphere of anger, sadness and hopelessness pervaded their camp.

Up above, said Scar, *you had to obey society's rules. Underground you can make your own rules. There are no mirrors. We don't need reflections down here.*

Scar and the rest of the tribe seemed convinced that the world was going to end; a holocaust of sorts. Society was too evil to keep functioning for very much longer.

After the apocalypse, said Scar, *we will be the ones who teach them upstairs how to survive. There's over 6000 of us. One day we will rise up.*

They were modern day troglodytes, who had a semblance of societal structure they had taken from the world above ground. The society had appointed runners whose job it was to occasionally make journeys to the surface in order to forage for food in garbage cans outside restaurants. A mayor was appointed as spokesman. Beneath the surface of the earth there were rival factions struggling for supremacy. There various ways to die down here. You could be struck by a train, or electrocuted by the dangerous 'third rail'. One mole person had recently gone out by peeing on said rail, with the stream of urine effectively serving as a live wire. Mole people died of natural causes too; AIDs, tuberculosis and pneumonia, and then there were the fights, the scraps, people stabbing each other with pen knives or beating each other to death with planks of wood. *Every day was a struggle for survival*, said Scar, who, as his name would suggest had a five inch scar down the right side of his face, like Scarface in the movie of the same name.

Many of the homeless were riddled with disease. AIDS, the common cold, pneumonia, tuberculosis, hypothermia and diabetes. Then there was the dangerous third rail which is a way of providing electric power to a train, by running a rigid conductor alongside the rails of a railway track. If a person touches the track they can have their hands, head or feet blown off. There are many derogatory terms to describe the homeless; derelicts, hobos, unseen or forgotten man, vagrants, bums, beggars. In Japan they are known as 'johatsu', which means 'wandering spirit' or a person who has lost his identity. These people are different; other.

Scar became my main friend amongst the mole people. He took me under his wing. Truth be told, he was the only one who demonstrated anything remotely resembling friendliness. The rest of them could be very standoffish, as if they considered me to be an invader, an intruder; a rich bitch who had decided to take a sojourn in the underworld in order to 'find material'. They were deeply suspicious of me, in the same way that a group of tigers will be suspicious of a lion that strays into their enclosure. I, in turn, was suspicious of Scar. Why was he being so friendly? Did he want something from me? Money? (I had none). Sex? (I was still a virgin and I certainly didn't intend to lose my cherry in a sewer.) These subway people referred to their home as 'Scum City' and they often joked amongst themselves about their poverty.

'What's that gorgeous scent you're wearing?' one sewer-dweller would say, sidling up to another in a parody of a New York socialite.

'Why, it's eau de rodent, darlink, the new must-have parfum for the ladies of New York.'

Or 'It's eau de turd, the very latest thing.'

Scar took to leaving me notes.

Gone rat-hunting. Back around 2pm.

Sometimes he went above ground in order to raid garbage cans or go binning (diving into clothes bins) for new threads. He often brought me home fresh finds – a T-shirt with the sleeves missing, a denim mini with white paint spattered on it, a pair of old trainers. I was grateful for these gifts and saw them as a sign of his growing affection, for Scar and I were getting closer all the time. He took me on a tour of the underground, through its empty tunnels, its disused ghost stations; City Hall, Brooklyn Bridge, Worth Street. There were clusters of mole people to be found at random intervals – rival factions. One group even had a microwave.

'One day soon we'll have internet access down here,' said Scar.

I wasn't sure whether it was a joke or not.

'Every now and then,' he continued, 'riots break out, one group pits itself against another.'

One day, one of the other subterranean dwellers tried to convince me to take drugs. Hammer caught him in the act of trying to get me to snort a line and kicked him in the arse. Hammer was a tough nut. He was African American and carried a hammer with him everywhere he went. He smashed objects, but not people, at random. Shards of glass, mirrors, an old drinking fountain. D-Dog was a failed rapper, but that didn't stop him from pumping out his so-called 'wicked rhymes' at every given hour of the night and day. He wore the mandatory backwards baseball cap and his jeans halfway down his bum, a tacky gold medallion and sneakers with the laces undone. Some of the mole people were more vulnerable than others. I know it may sound clichéd, and possibly sexist, but many of the women looked extremely fragile. Cindy in particular, a petite blonde woman, seemed very young and frail, permanently on the verge of breakdown. With time I got to know more about their backgrounds. They all had different reasons for wanting to live underground. Some of them couldn't afford to pay rent. Some were running away from abusive family members, or foster parents, or orphanages, or from the police. Many were addicted to booze, drugs and cigarettes and a large proportion suffered from some form of mental illness, depression or manic depression or schizophrenia. Nevertheless, despite their hardships, a large number of them were capable of forming supportive relationships and looking out for one another.

Given the choice, the vast majority of these subterranean dwellers would rather stay underground than return to a life on the surface. Above ground, they said, they were outcasts, invisibles, untouchables, alienated from friends and family. Underground, they had formed communities, cliques. They had a vision and a purpose, whether it be sweeping out their section of tunnel with a piece of old broom, or helping another mole person to give up the booze. What they had found here was a sense of belonging. Many of them claimed that they valued the human spirit above material comforts. Somewhat surprisingly, I found that these people had ethics, morals. To those who lived above ground, this existence seemed dystopian, but to most of the mole people they had found a slice of utopia. This was a tax haven, devoid of normal rules. Survival was all. This, claimed Scar, was really living. Here, the outsider became the insider. People infected with AIDS, or addicted to crack, or who had become mentally unstable were cared for. Many of the mole people had been abused at shelters; they'd either been raped or people had stolen from them and so they had fled into the bowels of the earth.

'The pigs come down here sometimes,' said Scar. 'They beat on us. Those bastards. *They're* the real vermin.'

It was Scar who introduced me to a man they called 'The Reader'. The Reader had brought his library down with him, dozens of leather-bound volumes, hard-backs and paperbacks. The Reader had a double degree in psychology and philosophy from Harvard. He had the obligatory grey beard and wore socks underneath his sandals. Special 'runners' were appointed to bring the mole people supplies from above ground. They brought The Reader fresh booty from local second-hand bookstores. The Reader was the main educator in the group. It was his duty to educate the subway's young. He taught them the three R's – reading, writing and arithmetic. In Scar's group there were only about six young people – ranging in age from three to eight. Mostly, they were well behaved, but every now and then, a couple of them would run riot and have to be quietened down by one of the older members of the group.

The Reader, in turn, introduced me to a man they called 'Black Angel.' Everybody was scared of Black Angel. He lived on his own in the bowels of the subway and was often to be found laughing and talking to himself and eating his own faeces. There was something deeply disturbing about him. It was as if he was possessed by a demon, or as if there was, in actuality, nobody inside him at all, as if he was soulless, empty, as hollow in the O in God. A nothingness in human form. I was too frightened to talk to Black Angel. I'm not sure what I thought he might do; stab me or eat me, barbeque me like one of those sewer rats that Scar and co were so fond of devouring.

Despite my best intentions regarding not losing my virginity in the subway, Scar and I soon started sleeping together. It started out as a comfort thing – somebody to cuddle up to on the cold winter nights. And also, entertainment. Something to do. The hours spent down in the subway were long and drawn out. Somebody had a small, battery-powered television they were always tuned into. There was a pack of dog-eared old cards and a tatty game of Monopoly.

Scar's friend Aran lived in the posh part of town – the condos. Here there were old mattresses, deck chairs, armchairs, a lamp hooked up with electricity wired from the train tracks and a gas cooker. By day we went out 'tagging' or graffiti writing. Scar tried to turn me into an Oliver Twist-style pickpocket during the day. I wasn't too keen on doing anything illegal. Scar did his best to persuade me that it was okay to smash people's windows and climb inside, but I remained unconvinced. I was a nice upper-class girl at heart. Mother and Father had raised me properly. I wouldn't descend to a life of crime so easily.

After I'd been living in the sewer for a couple of months, Scar took me out and taught me how to spear rats. He had a couple of old Indian spears. They had three bits of fur wrapped around them, and each piece of fur had two feathers stuck into it. When asked, he said he'd nicked them from a junk shop. We headed down into a sewer that branched out to the left and soon spotted a rat up ahead.

'Mickey Mouse's less adorable brother,' quipped Scar, as he stabbed his spear into its hind quarters.

He handed one of the spears to me. We headed further down the tunnel. I spied a rat.

'Gently, gently, catchee monkey,' warned Scar and I padded softly towards it.

I bought the spear down into the rat's hind quarters, in imitation of the way that Scar had impaled his catch of the day.

I became pregnant by Scar. My stomach expanded and expanded, pushing at the waistband of my trousers until they threatened to burst. The baby was born. We named it Fay. It had different coloured eyes, like David Bowie – one green, one blue. The poor thing cried and cried in the darkness until I gave in and took it 'upstairs' to where it could take in the light of day. Then it hushed up for while and quietened down and suckled calmly at my breast. Scar didn't think too much of the baby. There certainly wasn't a very strong father-daughter bond. He ignored it when it cried and ignored it when it laughed. I tried to shower the baby with adequate attention in order to make up for the ignoring.

The baby didn't grow especially fast due to the dark conditions underground. Its limbs were pale and withered. Just a smattering of blonde hair grew upon its head. Shortly after its third birthday, The Reader and I taught it to read. We started with *The Gruffalo,* which quickly became a favourite. Both Fay and I fell in love with the illustrations. We then moved on to *Room on the Broom* and *The Gruffalo's Child.* Over time Scar became more interested in Fay, but by that stage Fay had got the pip and didn't want anything to do with him.

From time to time Scar would speak to me of other underground factions in different cities. There were people living beneath the cities of Paris, LA and Las Vegas. How Scar knew this I'll never know. From newspapers maybe, or rumours. From the internet cafe that he sometimes visited on his rare trips above ground.

Due to the fact that Scar hadn't really bonded with Fay all that well, shortly after Fay's fourth birthday, I decided to venture back to life above ground. I had expected that Mother and Father would be glad to see me. Instead I found that they were furious.

"Where have you been?" they demanded. "And who have you been doing it with?"

"I've been underground," I said. "With the mole people." Of course, they didn't believe me. They thought I was making it up, fooling around. There was nothing that I could say or do that would make them take my word for it.

Mother instantly bonded with Fay. Fay smiled up at the family matriarch and mother was in love. Father wasn't quite so pleased.

"What the hell have you gone and gotten yourself up the duff for?" he asked in icy tones.

Maude swung by for a visit. She was chuffed to meet baby Fay as well. Her art works had finally started selling. Her formerly doomed career was finally starting to get off the ground.

A week later, Mother and I were out shopping in Bloomingdales when the super-storm hit – Hurricane Mandy. Climate change experts were saying that the storm was due to global warming. There was a five-metre high storm surge – five metres of water flooding into the subway. Which got me to thinking, maybe there could be further disturbed weather patterns on the way; hurricanes, tidal waves, acid rain, pea soup fog. Perhaps the end of the world was nigh; the Rapture, Apocalypse, Doomsday, Judgement Day. The storm dumped snow, brought down power lines and plunged the city into darkness. Tens of billions of dollars of damage were done. The power outages paralysed the nation. Chaos ensued. Seawater flooded the subway. There was no way to pump out the water. Ninety percent of the mole people were drowned. The other ten percent got warning and escaped. God only knows where they are now.

The Army brought in their water removal team. More than a dozen experts drained the tunnels, fishing out the bodies of drowned mole people as they went.

"They should have made the subways tsunami proof," I said to Mother, and she nodded her head in agreement.

"I wonder how many more of these storms are going to hit America," she pondered.

I thought about Scar's words.

After the apocalypse, we will be the ones who teach them upstairs how to survive. There's over six thousand of us. One day we will rise up.

A falsity. Five thousand of them had been drowned. The other thousand, however, were still on the loose, roaming free throughout New York and maybe, like cockroaches, with their hardened survival skills they would be the only things still alive after the final judgement had been delivered.

JACOB AND FIG

The giant lived deep in the woods in an enormous weta-ridden cave. The entrance was covered by fern fronds and moss, making it hard to find. He was a shy, gentle giant, not prone to eating children or partaking in any of the other horrendous activities giants are purported to do. He was lonely in his cave as he was the last of his kind, the others having died off long ago. His name was Fig and his mother had named him this when he was born because of his shape which was skinny at the top with a big bottom. When Fig was twelve years old his parents left him to go and look for others of their kind. They reasoned that he was old enough to fend for himself and, alone, Fig was forced to live on berries, fish from the stream and grubs from the forest floor.

Jacob Griffiths lived with his parents in a trailer park in Takaka, an hour and a half's drive from Nelson. He was a lonely boy - he was behind in his school work and he struggled to get on with others at school. People said he had a difficult personality. He was a loner, a lone wolf. His parents fought often – the atmosphere at home was fractious. When his parents fought Jacob would run away into the forest and explore. He would pretend he was in another world as a way of escaping the trauma he was experiencing at home. It was during one of these explorations that Jacob stumbled across Fig. He had seen the cave entrance, pushed aside the fern fronds and made his way inside. Fig was sitting on an upside down beer barrel he had salvaged from the nearby trailer park at night while everybody else was sleeping. Fig was nine foot tall with an enormous bottom. The cave had been chosen because it was large enough to accommodate him. Jacob looked startled when he saw Fig. He hadn't expected the cave to be inhabited. Fig felt disgruntled that somebody had entered his enclosure and it showed upon his face. He also felt frightened – his parents had told him to be scared of humans and all that they represented. There was a long silence. Jacob spoke first.

"Hello", he said, extending his hand. "I'm Jacob."

Fig didn't know anything about the human custom of shaking hands. He had lived alone in the forest since his parents had left him, and he stared at the extended hand without moving.

"Gosh *you're* big," said Jacob. How long have you been living here for then?"

The giant swallowed.

"Since I was young."

"With your parents?"

"No, they left."

"They left you on your own? That's not very responsible."

"Yes. They left to find others."

"What – and they didn't come back? What happened to them?"

"I never found out."

"Have you ever thought of looking for them?"

"No they told me to stay here – they said the world beyond wasn't safe."

"Oh that's just silly there's nothing dangerous about the world. Come on, why don't we go look for them."

The giant shrugged.

"Do you think it's safe out there? I've heard rumours of all sorts of nasties."

"It'll be fine. Just take my hand and we'll go looking for your parents."

Jacob held out his hand to the giant. After a pause, the giant took it.

"I've got a knife", said Jacob.

He took a hunting knife out of his backpack. The giant admired the sharp, shiny edge.

"What else have you got in there?" asked the giant.

Jacob took out some raisins, a rope, a compass, a whistle, some matches and a map of the area. The giant let go of Jacob's hand, went into his cave and came back out with some dehydrated rabbit's legs, a bow and arrow, a canvas and an animal trap. He put these into a bag that looked as if it was made from deer skin and slung it across his shoulder, then rose to his feet, towering over Jacob. They were outside the cave, in the fresh air. It was a crisp clear morning; there was a light frost and Jacob could see both his and the giant's breath.

They set off together into the woods. Small creatures scurried out of the way at their approach, and larger ones too, like pigs and deer. Fig promised Jacob that he would teach him how to hunt at a later date and Jacob said that he looked forward to it with eager anticipation. They followed animal tracks that Fig was able to locate easily enough and they also used Jacob's compass to head in the rough direction of North which was the direction that Fig said his parents had headed in when they had left. When they came to a river Fig fashioned a spear from a nearby branch using Jacob's hunting knife, and impaled a fresh fish, saying that they would cook it for lunch. They hiked for four hours and then it was time to cook.

Jacob lit a fire and cooked the fish. He split the creature in two and gave half to the giant. The giant ate his fish in a single gulp, bones and all. Down the hatch. Jacob carefully picked his off the bones, then threw the carcass into the bush.

Back at the trailer park, Jacob's parents began searching for him. They looked in the trailer park first and then, when he was not to be found there, they searched further afield, knocking on houses down the nearby streets and asking if anybody had seen their son. Nobody had seen hide nor hair of him. He had vanished without trace, disappeared into the ether. They were dead worried. They comforted one another with soothing words, but both were churning with anxiety underneath.

After three hours of searching they went home, telling themselves that they would file a missing persons report in the morning. They would give him the evening and the night to return home of his own accord but if he wasn't there by dawn they would be forced to take action. Jacob's parents fought often, mostly because they had no money and this was just one more worry piled upon their already full plate.

Fig and Jacob finished their lunch. They hiked on in relative silence for another three hours. Jacob imagined he could hear the trees talking.

Saw them come this way, whispered the trees. *They walked this way.*

Eventually, the bush started to clear and Jacob realized they had come to one of Golden Bays many beaches. He did not know what bay they were at but he pointed at the water and said, 'Look Fig, the ocean.' Fig smiled, then said 'What's all those black shapes on the beach.' Jacob looked again more closely. Fig was right. Stranded on the beach was a pod of whales. It was a melancholy sight. Jacob hated to see animals in trouble. Various townspeople were down on the beach pouring buckets of water over the animals and trying to get them back out to sea. Somebody had a tractor.

"Fig can help," said Fig and bounded down to where the whales lay.

When he reached the area where the whales lay he began making a series of high pitched noises – whale squeaks, sonar with patches of silence. The whales seemed to be listening. Remarkably, with some assistance from the people on the beach they began to roll, over and over, towards the ocean, towards freedom. Fig worked with the whales for over four hours, until every last one was safely swimming back out to sea.

When he had finished there was a round of applause. He was the hero of the hour.

"Here buddy, let me buy you a beer", offered somebody, clapping him on the back.

Fig looked to Jacob for guidance.

"He wants to buy you a drink", explained Jacob. "To say thanks."

"No thanks", said Fig. "I go too."

As Jacob stood on the beach and watched, he waded in up to his thighs, then up to his chest and then began swimming, following the whales. Jacob watched in astonishment as Fig began to transform himself from human into whale – first his legs changed into a tail, then his head took the shape of a whale - a blow hole must have opened up on top of his head because Jacob saw a fine spray of water come shooting up out of it. He swam, further and further out to sea and Jacob had the sad feeling that he would never see Fig again.

Maybe that's what happened to his parents, he thought to himself, wondering if the giants were somehow descended from whale stock.

Only then, when he was alone, did Jacob begin to think about his parents. He had not left them a note. They would be missing him. He knew that his folks didn't have much money, but he was just a kid, what could he do about it. A milk run or a paper round wouldn't make much difference. He could buy a lotto ticket and hope for the best, but what were the chances? Him and a million other hopefuls could dream on. He walked past the WINZ office; he knew that his Mum had been in there many times. There was a notice up in the window; *Assistance provided to start small businesses. Make an appointment.* A small business would be perfect for his family. It could help them get off the ground. He stayed the night in Takaka at a backpackers using pocket money that he had saved up. He liked feeling like an adult, although he was a little scared, as he had never been away from his parents for this long without another relative.

The next morning he caught the bus back to the trailer park. He headed for home, feeling sad that he had lost the one friend he had found. He arrived at the trailer to find his mother in a state.

"Where the hell have you been? I've been worried sick. You can't just take off without letting us know where you're going."

"You were fighting. I'm sick of the fights."

"That's no excuse", she said, then softened and put her arm around his shoulders. "O love, I know life's tough for you. We don't have much money and you've got no friends."

"I've been thinking Mum. You could start a small business. WINZ are offering grants. What about a leisure park at one of the bays?"

She lit a cigarette and stared hard at him.

"What the hell are you on about now?"

"Come on Mum. There's got to be a better future for us than being stuck in this dump."

"Whispering Pines Trailer Park is luxury accommodation thank you very much young man. You should be grateful to have a roof over your head."

"A small business is a good opportunity Mum. And Dad could stop working those long hours for crap pay at the recycling centre."

"I'll talk to your father about it. Anyway, stop changing the topic - where the hell have you been?"

"Well Mum", said Jacob. "I've been on quite an adventure…"

THE RIVER

Kylie Sampson had been living with brain cancer – an oligodendroglioma to be precise, for four years. She'd had a craniotomy, but they'd not got all of it. There were days when she felt horribly depressed, knowing that she had a terminal illness and on these days she would take herself to the river and reflect. The river was calm and deep and Kylie would stare into it for hours. She was up the river one day when she crossed paths with an older man who had a stack of books on his lap. She approached him tentatively and he extended his right hand with a book in it, held out to her as a gift. The book was entitled 'Life's Labyrinth' and it had a red cover with gold etching. It was well worn as if he had carried it around and kept it close to him for years, ready to give to the right person. Kylie opened up the book. It fell open to the middle pages and a passage of highlighted text sprung out at her.

The river carries us in unexpected directions.

The key is to accept the flow.

Kylie had been struggling to come to terms with her cancer. Before being diagnosed she had been a teacher at Fairfield Kindergarten. She'd had to lose her whole career. When the tumour had first started to grow she had gone to her local GP who had dismissed her symptoms as 'psychological'. Further investigations, and an MRI scan, had revealed a cancerous mass growing on her left frontal lobe, a dark evil tumour, threatening her sanity and her life. She'd begun to suffer seizures which left her disorientated and confused. Afterwards, the world seemed gelatinous, like jelly. Kylie hated her tumour. It had taken so much from her; her career, her spark, her hopes for the future. She wanted life to be back the way that it had been, pre-cancer, when she had worked with Cindy, Shelly and Susan at the kindergarten and they had shared a laugh together during break time. Now she was stuck at home all the time, unable to work due to fatigue, confusion and memory problems. She'd got into big trouble for leaving little Johnny unattended three months ago. He had run out onto the road and nearly got hit by a truck. She had been looking around for other hobbies to fill her time, but nothing had cropped up. She'd had a craniotomy, which had been a physical success but a psychological disaster. The operation was traumatic. They'd taken a tumour the size of three walnuts out of her left frontal lobe. She'd had a brain haemmorage, and felt that she had come close to dying. She'd seen a DVD of her own funeral played out on the TV screen in the hospital – an hallucination caused by seizure activity. After the surgery she had suffered nightmares of being buried alive, trapped, helpless, unable to move.

"You are the girl in my dream", the old man said to her. "I saw you having a successful exhibition. You were a sculptor."
Kylie was skeptical. She didn't believe in dreams. She was a practical, no-nonsense kind of girl who thought that hard work was what got you places. The only problem was that she couldn't work hard anymore, not now, so she needed something else to occupy her days. She thought that sculpting would be perfect to fill the void.

The following week she set out to buy the supplies she would need. She bought powdered clay in a bag, sculpting tools and a plastic apron. She worked in the garage at the back of her flat. Kylie did not live alone and for this she was grateful. Her life would have been awfully lonely post-diagnosis had it not been for her

45

flatmates. They kept her company and tried to cheer her up and she was always grateful for their lively voices echoing about the house. They had agreed that she could have space in the garage to do her work.

Kylie set up her equipment by the window where the natural light shone through. She sculpted the face of the old man first, then the faces of her flatmates. She moved onto river creatures; a trout, a dragonfly and an eel. The light began to fade. She looked down at her watch. Time had flown by – she had been so engrossed in her work that she had not noticed the passing of time. She put the pieces she had created to one side, where she could come back and look at them another day. During the time she had been sculpting, she hadn't thought of her dreadful diagnosis once, and when she looked at her work she felt a sense of pride in what she had accomplished.

She went inside and joined her flatmates who were playing Scrabble. When she looked down at the Scrabble board she saw that the words 'river' and 'eel' were laid out there. She felt that she was moving in the right direction and that maybe the tumour was not the terrible curse she had at first thought it was. Money was tight for Kylie – she lived on an invalid's benefit and had done since losing her teaching job. Luxuries were few and far between. She cooked big curries of lentils and cauliflower, chickpeas and pumpkin and lived on them for weeks on end. She did not have grandiose ambitions for herself as a sculptor – she just hoped to hold a small local exhibition and maybe to sell a few pieces. Money was not the main motivator. Sculpting was the direction she now found herself moving in. She would just have to see where it took her.

What Kylie liked most about sculpting was the fact that she could lose herself in her work and forget about her everyday worries and cares when she was working.　The problems that threatened to swamp and drown her diminished as soon as she had her hands in the clay.　Sculpting helped her to gain much-needed perspective.

That night when Kylie was in bed asleep she dreamt she was half-woman, half-eel, swimming happily down the river, past the old man, past some fishermen on the riverbank, weaving through a school of trout that were coming in the opposite direction, following the river out to the sea.

THE NEW VALVE

Faulty hearts run in my family. My father had to have a valve replaced by a pig valve when he was in his early thirties and my uncle died of a heart attack in his fifties. I work at a MDF plant in Nelson and my own heart is enlarged. Two weeks ago they discovered that the valve wasn't working properly and was only letting through 9% of the blood flow. I was admitted to Nelson hospital and they told me they were going to fly me to Wellington to do open heart surgery and replace the valve. At first they said they were going to use a pig's valve like they did with Dad but then they changed their minds and said I was too young, forty-three, and that a pig's valve would not last me for life and that they would use a titanium one instead. I was a non smoker. The dud heart was just a card in the hand I had been dealt.

My girlfriend Kerry likes to make a fuss of me and she was hovering around the hospital during the days before I was due to fly out to Wellington. My parents look down their snobby noses at her because she's a solo mother and does not have much money, so there was a bit of tension there. I tried to ease the atmosphere by cracking jokes, even though I wasn't in much of a laughing mood, lying flat on my back in Nelson hospital, wondering when they were going to fly me to Wellington and whether or not the operation was going to be a success, but I tried to lighten things up a little. Kerry is a sensitive soul who likes to be liked and she did not take kindly to my parents snobbery. "They're judging me", she told me. "And they haven't even taken the time to get to know the real me. They're just judging me on my exterior. It's not fair. I'm a good, kind person. I'm not after your money. I help take care of you. I care about what happens to you. I'm caring all round."

My parents did not seem to notice kind and caring. They noticed money and status and what job a person was able to hold down. Kerry worked for the DHB as a support worker helping a lady who'd had a brain tumour removed, but that wasn't good enough for my folks.

They flew me out to Wellington on a Sunday. It was windy and raining and I was dreading what lay ahead. Donald Trump's military had dropped the 'mother of all bombs' on Isis tunnels in Afghanistan the night before. He had ordered a tomahawk cruise missile strike on Syria a few days previous to this and earlier in the year there had been a military raid of an al-Qaida affiliate complex in Yemen. Trump was proving himself to be quite the war monger and people were saying that he would go down in history as the 'war president'. I wasn't sure how I felt about being alive during the reign of such an aggressive and war hungry president, even if New Zealand was located half a world away at the bottom of the South Pacific. They said the bomb was the biggest non nuclear bomb ever used in combat. I watched footage of the testing of such a bomb online and I thought of the people whose lives had been destroyed. The US claimed that only members of Isis had been killed but I thought that this was bullshit. The dropping of the bomb made me feel small, powerless and insignificant, as if my life too could be snuffed out in an instant. The Pink Floyd song 'Mother' kept playing in the back of my mind. The bombing made me extra nervous before my big operation. After all, they were going to saw through my chest and breast bone and operate on my heart, the muscle that kept me ticking, kept the blood pumping through my body. It would only take one slip of the surgeon's blade and it would be all over for me too, lights out, game over. *Died on the operating table*, they would write on my death certificate. Or *died in theatre.*

I was disturbed by Donald Trump and his actions. What did it mean that America had voted him in? Or had it been not so much a vote *for* Donald as a vote *against* Hilary and therefore a sign that America was still deeply sexist. I didn't have the answers but that didn't stop the questions from forming in my mind.

An orderly from the hospital met my flight and took a taxi with me from the airport to the hospital. They settled me into Ward 6 South. To one side of me lay Wayne, who was having a triple bypass and to the other side lay Karen, a smoker, who was having a tumour removed from her lung. All fun and games in Ward 6 South. Somebody had sent Karen a bunch of flowers – pink lilies, the colour of a healthy set of lungs and somebody else had tied a Get Well Soon balloon to the end of Wayne's bed. All this false cheer and heartiness just made my own situation seem worse – my own bed and area was unadorned. Still, I had only just arrived. There was still time.

My thoughts turned to my girlfriend Kerry and I wondered if she would send me anything – a card, some chocolates or some blooms. Kerry was taking a paper in Advanced Fiction through Massey University and one of the stories they'd had to read was Stephen King's 'Autopsy Room 4'. I'd read the story too and it had scared the beejesuz out of me. It's about a man who's been paralysed by a snake. He is pronounced dead but gains consciousness but can't speak or move right before they are about to perform an autopsy on him. Not the kind of story you'd want to think of right before a big operation.

I had brought my laptop with me. I asked an orderly if I could have a password for the wifi so I could keep up with world news and distract myself from thinking about 'Autopsy Room 4'. She obliged and said 'you take it easy now, don't over exert yourself. You've got the big operation coming up tomorrow.' I smiled and nodded, then logged on.

By now, Donald Trump had redirected a 'very powerful' naval armada to the Korean peninsula and was telling North Korea that they were 'looking for trouble' via Twitter. Sabre rattling. Displaying military might. Some people said that by bombing Afghanistan Trump was sending a message to Kim Jong-un in North Korea, although the president denied this. Down here, down South, I was lying in wait for my Big Op, up there, in the Northern Hemisphere, two megalomaniacs postured and strutted on the world's stage. There was no doubt that terrorism and North Korea posed grave threats to the world, but was Trump's solution – more war, really a decent one? Still, what would my solution be? To sit down with a few members of al-Qaida and a translator over a chai latte and have a rational discussion about a peaceable solution to the problem? Probably get my head blown off. My father always said that Americans considered themselves to be the cops of the world – was Trump now playing police commissioner? In my chest, the faulty valve flapped to and fro, struggling to do its job.

I signed a consent form the following morning. A nurse came and took me to a sterile hospital bathroom. She stripped me off and shaved my stomach, chest and arms with a puny Bic razor.

I was taken back to my ward which had a window overlooking the hospital carpark. I was gazing out the window, bored with my current sudoku, when I saw a flash looking Lexus SUV LX pull up in the parking lot. The door on the driver's side opened and a tall dark haired man with a confident stride stepped out. He strode towards the hospital's main doors – a man with a purpose. Ten minutes later he was standing beside my bed, introducing himself to me as my surgeon.

"Hello I'm Graeme Young", he said with a smile. "I understand we're dealing with stenosis of the aortic valve."
I nodded grimly.
"It's not entirely my fault", I said. "I'm not the world's healthiest eater but it's also partly hereditary and partly due to stress. Job stress mostly. I'm a non smoker."
"I see."
A nurse entered the room.
"Is everything under control?" she asked.
"Sure", replied Graeme smoothly. "Leave this one in my capable hands."
He winked.
The wink made me feel uneasy. Surely surgery was a serious business and not something to be winked about.

The surgeon left the room and I was left alone with the TV and my sudoku. The TV was tuned into world news which was all about Trump and his naval armada, including a nuclear powered submarine which had been sent to the Korean peninsula. I thought it was a bit ironic that he had sent a nuclear powered submarine considering that he was so vocal in his disdain for North Korea and their nuclear weapons. Google also informed me that the United States had 1500 nuclear arms whereas North Korea was estimated to have only around 20. I felt short of breath and my heart began to palpitate at the thought of all those nukes.

A nurse came and took me in a room next to theatre. She showed me the consent form and asked me to confirm that it was my signature. The anesthetist came and introduced himself to me as Karl Maine. I felt far from psychologically ready, everything was happening so fast. They wheeled me into theatre. The anesthetist put a needle in my arm and that is the last thing I remember for a while.

So were you on your own last night, I heard a voice saying. I thought at first that somebody was talking to me. I tried to talk but there was something stuck down my throat.
It must be the breathing tube, I thought to myself.
I wondered if the operation was over and if they had just mistakenly left the breathing tube in.
Oh look this guy's heart is really enlarged, check it out. It's massive.
This time I recognized the voice of the surgeon. How could he be looking at my heart? I was awake, conscious. Surely they couldn't still be operating on me. It was like a nightmare. I attempted to open my eyes but it was as if my lids were stuck shut with Superglue.
Time for the valve please, I heard the surgeon say.
There was a tinkle of metal on metal, the titanium valve on its tray. I couldn't feel anything yet I could hear everything. I was paralysed and could not open my eyes to signal to anybody that I was awake. I felt helpless – an insect trapped in amber. There was a mechanical

humming noise in the background – I assumed it was emanating from the heart lung machine. Why had I regained partial consciousness? Did this mean that the anesthetic had partially worn off or had I not been given the correct dose? If I had come round to this point, did this mean that I was going to regain further feeling? I had researched a little about heart surgery and I knew that they stopped the heart. Had I died during the surgery? Was I now a ghost – was that why I could hear what was going on? Had Kim Jong-un dropped a nuclear bomb on Australia during my operation? Had North Korea been far further ahead in the nuclear game that anybody had realized? The cold hand of panic gripped my bloodless heart. The only other time I had ever felt so helpless was when I was seven years old and my elder cousin gagged me and tied me up and left me in the wardrobe on Christmas Day, then went down to have dinner with the adults.

Alright the valve's in, time to stitch this guy up.

I imagined the needle and thread running through my heart, stitch by stitch, holding me together.

Wire up his sternum, was the next instruction that reached my woozy ears.

I tried to indicate with one hand that I was conscious but my brain would not send signals to my muscles. If only I could twitch a foot! Why had the anesthetic worn off? Were the people in charge of my operation a bunch of nincompoops? Was it going to wear off any further? Was I going to start to feel pain – the pain of a dead, still heart? A female voice spoke.

Hang on a minute, I saw an eyelid twitch. He's not under properly. Karl do your bloody job. We need you to concentrate.

O shit, sorry about that, came the muttered reply. *I'll just increase the dose.*

So I *was* dealing with a bunch of amateurs! Damned New Zealand medical system. Hadn't these people had a decent education? Hadn't they been trained? The operation was almost over and *now* they were worrying about putting me back under.

The next thing I knew I was waking up in a stark bare hospital ward. I was pretty doped up on morphine when the surgeon came around to see me with a nurse in tow. Despite the morphine, I still managed to spit my story out. I was angry. Why hadn't the anesthetist done his job properly?

"And how is our patient doing today?"

"Not good. Why did I come to during the surgery. I can remember large chunks of it. I can remember your voice issuing instructions and then a female voice said that I wasn't under properly and that she had seen an eyelid twitch. What sort of mickey mouse outfit are you running here?"

The surgeon laughed as the nurse fidgeted.

"Oh sometimes our patients have these hallucinations when they're under. It's an effect of the anesthetic."

"Bullshit. I know what I heard."

My throat was sore from where the breathing tube had been stuffed down but I was determined to have my say. The surgeon patted my hand.

"Don't fret. You've been through a traumatic experience, it's normal to be a bit confused. Your girlfriend rang and she says she's made everything nice for you at home."

His beeper went off.

"Oh, I'm a wanted man. Gotta dash."

He headed off down the corridor with the nurse following in his wake.

I stayed in the ward for another week. Kerry called every night. I was glad to hear her voice; it was good to hear something that reminded me of Nelson. I had been told that I could not return to work for four months following the surgery so I would be spending a lot of time at my home, reading and walking on the beach trying to recover from my big operation.

One of the nurses instructed me to get up and walk around as much as I could. I traipsed the corridors, back and forth, a lonely ghost, and then ventured out into the stairwell.

On the day they discharged me I went to the men's room to relieve my bladder. I heard a familiar voice coming from the direction of the urinal.

"God that was a great party the other night. Got so wasted I could barely stand the next day. Still came into work though. Didn't want to risk losing my job. Did an open heart surgery that morning."

I quickly flushed the toilet and came out into the main room, just in time to see the anesthetist zipping up his fly. I didn't say anything but at least I'd had my suspicions confirmed.

I flew back to Nelson the following day. Kerry had made the house into a home, triangle pillows on the bed and everything. Against my parents wishes Kerry moved into the house with me to provide maximum care – she still kept her job. I was on Warfarin and pain killers. The Warfarin made me bruise easily. I was so traumatized by what had happened that for the first two months after the surgery all I did was lie in bed all day clutching a stuffed bear named Fuzzy that Kerry had bought for me. My mother was very concerned and sent me to the doctor for a dose of anti-depressants. What I felt was not depression but fear and anxiety. How could so-called 'trusted medical professionals' get it so wrong? Why had the anesthetist been allowed to go in to work – did nobody notice the state he was in before the operation? Why had such an irresponsible person been employed? Eventually Kerry managed to coax me out for walks at the beach followed by a cup of hot chocolate. These walks – and the chocolate reward became a daily routine for us, and something I looked forward to each day. We would do a loop – along the front beach and then around the back beach where people walk their dogs – to the café.

Although it might sound childish, I also played a lot of games in order to keep my brain working. Catan, Agricola, Discworld, Cluedo and First Around the World. Work had said that they would hold my position open for me for four months, to give me time to recover. You can't sue a medical professional in New Zealand but Kerry said I should write to the Health and Disability Commissioner and make an official complaint. I wrote in stating that I had gained consciousness during the surgery and then later, after the operation, overheard the anesthetist boasting about how drunk or stoned he had been the night before. My letter was acknowledged with a perfunctory slip and then eight weeks later I received a note stating that the anesthetist no longer worked at the hospital and that no charges would be pressed.

Fat lot of good that did, I thought to myself. *So much for justice.*

I cursed my bad genes for my faulty heart. Towards the end of the four months I found myself looking forward to going back to work, back to some sense of normalcy, back to structure and routine. Aren't these all that keep a man from floundering in the abyss? Kerryn had a few books lying around the house and I recognized one as being the short story collection that contained *Autopsy Room 4*, but I dared not open it up and read the story for a second time.

I suffered recurring nightmares, the worst of which was that I was back in hospital being operated upon by Donald Trump. No amount of walking at the beach could take my nightmares away. As for Donald Trump, he had calmed down a bit and was even talking about conciliatory talks with Kim Jong Un. However, all the bombs they possessed between them played upon my mind. The nukes were like a time bomb, ticking away like the titanium valve that was implanted in my heart.

WHITE LOTUS

Kerryn Jacobs saw the white lotus first in a book on Singapore that she had checked out from the library. Something about the image spoke to her and she could not clear it from her mind. It kept cropping up, unbidden. When she looked upon its beauty she was filled with hope for her future. At home, she Googled 'white lotus' to see what she could find out about its meaning. She discovered that the flower was symbolic in Hinduism and Buddhism because it comes from muddy water yet is itself pristine and beautiful. When one reaches the state of the white lotus it is said that they have attained mental purity and spiritual perfection. The flower is also linked with the pacification of one's own nature.

Kerryn was an English Honours student studying at Auckland University. She lived in Point Chevalier with two flatmates, one of whom was an engineering student and the other who worked full-time in a bar in Britomart. Kerryn made up her mind to get a tattoo of the lotus upon her wrist and made the journey to busy K-road one Saturday morning to visit a tattoo parlour. A couple of hookers were loitering outside the shop. She took the book on Singapore with her. The man behind the counter was burly and covered in tattoos.   Tats were also displayed upon the walls; Kerryn could not see a white lotus on show but she had her book which she clutched tightly to her chest.

"Hello, can I help you?" spoke the man.

His voice was gravelly and Kerryn felt a little afraid of him. She didn't come down K-road often. She gathered her courage.

"I…I've come for a tattoo", she said, holding out the book with the page open at the picture of the lotus.

"Got something in mind have ya?"

"Yes, I'd like that lotus upon my wrist. Just a bud. Not yet opened. Do you think you can do that?"

The man scoffed.

"I can do anything sweetheart."

Kerryn winced. She hated being called 'sweetheart.'

"Got thirty years experience", boasted the man.

He took the book from her hands.

"Now let's see the picture of this flower you want done."

He studied the picture for a while.

"White ink. Should be okay on your dark skin."

Kerryn was part Maori.

"Follow me out the back."

Kerryn dutifully trotted behind the man to a room at the rear of the shop. He gestured towards a chair and she took a seat. He got out his equipment and began to tattoo her wrist. Kerryn watched as the lotus bud took shape; the white blossom and then the leaves. She was silent throughout the course of the procedure. It felt like being stabbed with a hot matchstick. An hour and a quarter later, the tattooist was done. Kerryn looked down at her wrist. The lotus bud sat there, quiet and serene. She paid for the tattoo and left the shop, happy with the morning's proceedings.

The following week she was in a bar in Newtown and was showing somebody the tattoo when she noticed that it had sprouted three new leaves and an extra shoot out each side. She exclaimed out loud.

"Hey, my tattoo's grown shoots!"

A couple of people turned to look.

The man she was with grabbed her wrist for a closer look.

"Was it really smaller than this when you got it? Are you sure you're not just imagining things?"

"Yes those leaves are new and those sprouts to each side. It's grown. How mysterious. How amazing."

Kerryn began to take special care of the tattoo. She washed it with an expensive clay and spirulina soap and moisturized it with kowhai flower and sweet orange moisturizer. It rewarded her with extra growth – two new leaves and a bud. It tingled when it grew. The old bud had begun to open, showing its golden heart to the world. Kerryn was excited by the new growth but also a little freaked out and full of questions. Was the tattoo magic? Why was it growing? Was it ever going to stop or would it take over her entire body until she was covered in lotus blossom?

Kerryn was assigned a difficult essay topic; choose a Shakespeare play, discuss the works it has come from and then relate the play to a modern day adaptation. Kerryn had been struggling with the topic. She had chosen 'Taming of the Shrew' –referencing Thomas Kyd's **The Spanish Tragedy and** *Lodovico Ariosto* **as source material** and 'Kiss Me Kate' as a modern day adaptation. She wrestled with the topic for four hours one evening, then went online, googled and found an essay that was close enough to what she wanted written by an American student. She downloaded the essay, changed some of the text and submitted it as her own work.

The lecturer did not cotton on but the lotus knew. It shed three leaves and two of the buds lost their gloss and began to droop. Kerryn felt guilty, sad and ashamed that she had cheated and apologised to the lotus as if it was a real person who could hear her.
"I'm sorry", she said. "I just got stuck. I needed help."
The lotus was silent, said nothing.

Kerryn did her best to lead a good wholesome life to please the lotus and keep it happy. She wanted its leaves and buds to be glossy, she wanted it to continue growing. Prior to getting her tattoo she had been fighting a lot with her boyfriend, petty little tennis match arguments, batting the ball back and forth and getting nowhere, claws extended. Kerryn began making a special effort to ensure relations with her boyfriend, Darryl, were more harmonious. She cooked special dinners for the two of them to share and made more time and space for him in her life. She had previously been so wrapped up in her studies that she had only been able to allocate him small chunks of herself. She began to be more generous, meeting him after lectures and spending whole evenings with him in a bar or restaurant.

One evening they were getting on particularly well. Their fights had become a thing of the past and they were chatting together in a bar in Britomart. Darryl was a drama student and he was telling Kerryn about a part he had snagged in *Midsummer Night's Dream*. He was over the moon because he had won the right to play the character Oberon. He was flying high, especially after a couple of drinks. Kerryn liked him when he was like this; happy and free, settled in his studies, content in his life. He was an excellent actor, hard working and dedicated and she felt that he could 'go places' when he had completed his studies. He was building contacts, 'networking' – wasn't that what you were supposed to do? She didn't want to see him crash and burn and end up on the dole or waiting tables full-time with no time to pursue his dreams, like so many others.

That night, in the shower, she looked down at her skin. The lotus was glossy, almost glowing. Then, something amazing happened. One of the buds that was not yet opened, spread its petals and a dragonfly flew out and buzzed around the bathroom for a couple of laps before heading out the window. Kerryn stared in astonishment. The tattoo was bewitched! The man who had given it to her was a wizard, a magician, hiding out on ordinary K-road. The world was full of astonishment.

To assuage her guilt, Kerryn decided to re-do the Shakespeare essay. She asked for a deadline extension and this was granted. She applied herself to the topic, sitting in the library for hours on end. By the end of June she was satisfied with her completed project and she handed it in to the lecturer. It felt like a weight had been lifted.

She received an A- for the essay and she was more than happy with the mark. It had been a difficult topic and at least, in the end, she had not plagarised – it had been her own original work that she had handed in. She felt that the lotus was bringing her good luck.

Other creatures came forth from it. One morning a bee flew out and on another occasion a butterfly came flapping into the open. It was a spectacle, a miracle. It had grown prodigiously and now covered over half her body; her left arm, half her chest, her left leg and her neck. It was on display during the day and people commented on it.

"Gosh, isn't that an interesting tattoo you've got. So unique."

"What *is* that flower. It looks so familiar, yet I can't quite place what it is."

Kerryn wanted to speak with the man who had given her the tattoo to see if she could get to the bottom of its mysteries. She returned to where the shop had been at four pm the following Monday. The shop was nowhere to be found; there was just empty space where it had been, a vacant lot.

CHRISTMAS ISLAND

I know it's not Hiroshima, but my uncle was at Christmas Island when the Valient dropped the H-bomb. The crew were instructed by the officers to turn their backs to the bomb and to cover their eyes with their hands. The explosion was so bright that the crew could see right through the skin and flesh of their hands to the bone, like an X-ray. Their skeletons lit up. Moments later, they were told to rise to their feet and turn to face the blast. A mushroom cloud gathered on the far horizon. Some people were knocked to the ground. Birds lost their eyesight. Panes shattered. Trees lost their leaves.

Many of the servicemen developed cancer and other ailments such as diabetes. Claims were made to the government and widows who were down on their luck were paid a small pension – not enough to compensate them for the loss of their husbands but still, it was something. My uncle died early; aged fifty-five. There could have been other factors involved in his death, of course – his heavy smoking and drinking, his steady diet of fish and chips.

It's an image I can't shake from my mind – the skin covering the hands and the eyelids becoming transparent. The five fingers of the hand, white, skeletal, outlined against the sky - the blast much brighter than the sun.

THE SAMMY SERIES

Sammy

I fell from the sky on a Tuesday. Came down full of piss and thunder, but terrified too, *what the hell was happening?* I was a rebel angel. Once on earth I donned dark glasses and tight black jeans, rode a Harley, and obtained two tattoos. On my left arm, a dragon, on my right, a white lotus. People were scared of me, an effect I did not mind. I felt like a god in disguise. I picked up a mini-skirted girlfriend called Tiffany with an eighties perm and a lip piercing and I was set. Planet Earth? I thought I owned the place.

I was God's gift to women; a tiger in the sack. My pet hatred? Red lights. Didn't see the point in them. Wrote to the council about it - *Dear Mr So and So* - never got a bloody reply, damned if I could figure out why. So I just started running right through them; rules were made to be broken. Nobody got hurt – that in itself was a miracle.

I was a lone wolf, too proud to belong to any gang. I operated solo. I had my own batchelor pad, complete with rotating heart shaped bed and mirrors on the ceiling. Tiffany made a great custom made duvet cover with a tiger on it and fluffy blue trim. There was a bar in one corner of the bedroom and a bar in the lounge too. Blue LED lights were on display throughout the house. A finishing touch.

Money? Luckily for me Tiffany was loaded. Her Dad was a banker in the city and sent her a big fat cheque every month. She was very generous – she helped me afford my pad. In the back of my mind, I had a vague inkling that I had been sent to earth for a purpose. When I saw a rock musician on stage I would feel guilty that I had somehow let the side down. There had been another aspect to this mission on earth and it had involved music. Unfortunately, I had not mastered any instrument, in fact, I hadn't mastered anything at all, apart from making Tiffany giggle.

I know it might sound crazy but one night the Big Fella appeared to me in a dream. I can't really recall what he was saying 'cause I was half-smashed but it was something along the lines of *pull your socks up buddy or you'll be going back where you came from.* Course I didn't pay it any mind. Just a stupid dream.

But bugger me days if the next week I wasn't driving home from the pub when I took one red light too many and came face to face with the grill of a logging truck. Lights out. Game over.

Tiffany

Sammy picked me up at the pub one Saturday night. It wasn't love at first sight but there was something different about him. Maybe it was the tattoos. He didn't act like most guys so I was intrigued. He sure had one hell of an ego. He thought he was fantastic between the sheets but between you me and the gatepost he didn't seem to have much experience and many was the time I went away unsatisfied. I don't think he realized that making love involves *two* people – he was selfish and lazy; as long as he got his rocks off he was happy. So why was I with him? It was the Harley that did it for me. Such a beautiful bike? So sleek, so powerful, such thrust in the engine and the speed! I was often on the back of the bike. Sammy would break the red lights and I would have kittens, but it gave me a thrill too.

I didn't know where Sammy had come from. He didn't talk at all about his past. I wondered if he had been a criminal. It was as if he'd just appeared from thin air; I'd never seen him round in the pub before and I knew almost everybody in our neck of the woods. God he was a bludger. Didn't work, didn't even try to find a job, didn't know what CV meant – just sat around smoking, drinking and playing air guitar all day. One time I caught him at it and he was dead embarrassed. I hooked him up with an apartment to get him out of my house, out of my hair. My Dad's loaded, sends me monthly payments for my hairdressing business. I specialize in eighties perms.

He used to have weird dreams and mumble in his sleep like he was talking to somebody and one time I heard him say something about his socks. The relationship didn't last long. Things ended tragically. We were fighting about the money I give him and I accused him of being a bludger. Of course I feel real guilty about it now that he's gone. He took off on his bike in a mood – raced away with a screech of tyres and a fag in his mouth.

Half an hour later, the cops came knocking at the door and I ran around hiding Sammy's drugs but when I answered it turns out they were just there to break some terrible news.

"Do you know Sammy?"

Nobody knew his last name. I don't think he had one.

"Yes", I said. "He is my boyfriend. What's he done now?"

"I'm afraid there's been an accident. Sammy hit a logging truck this afternoon. He's no longer with us."

I burst into tears – couldn't help myself. God I'm gonna miss that Harley.

Tiffany's Dream

Sammy was hardly cold in his grave when he appeared to me in a dream. He was against a backdrop of clouds that looked like they were made out of cotton wool and there was gold glitter sprinkled all around him. Looked like some schoolkid's project and I thought to myself *O come on Sammy you can do better than that.* Lazy, even in the afterlife. Like all angels he bore a message. *Hey sweetheart, your hairdressing gig's gonna go tits up if you don't stop doing those ridiculous eighties perms. You need to move on. Get with the times.* I took it as a warning; a sign from above and I was grateful to Sammy for the tip.

I had to diversify. Next day I went to the library and searched high and low for the book "Peroxide for Dummies" - I'd seen it before, when I was a student, I'd had an idea I was going to become Peroxide Queen of London - thank you Sammy for providing just the inspiration I needed. I took the book into work but hid it behind the counter so people didn't know I was a novice. How hard could it be? My first victim was a wannabe model, eighteen years old and full of herself. Chloe was the name. Wanted 'golden highlights' whatever the hell that means. I bunged on the peroxide and left it for three hours so it would be good and done. Went and had a long leisurely lunch with my friends. Came back and rinsed her off – I must admit I noticed a certain amount of 'golden highlights' heading down the plughole but I didn't pay it any mind. She paid up so I was happy. The next day the poor lamb came back in tears demanding her money back, muttering that her modelling career was over. I couldn't hear her clearly through the sobs. I told her I never did refunds. She said she'd 'get even' whatever the hell that means.

After that we had a boy band called 'Dicks Forever!' – they thought that the name empowered the penis, but most people took it another way. They all had short spikey hair and wanted frosted tips. I got out the tinfoil. Wrapped them all up nice and neat and went next door to see my mate at Nails 'R Us and get my nails done. Came back and rinsed them all off. Success!! They went away smiling and laughing and I gave myself a mental pat on the back and said *Good job Tiff.*

The next morning I turned up to work and Dicks Forever! were sitting outside my parlour looking grumpy. They took their hats off in unison. Green tips!! I was flabbergasted. I could not be held responsible for this.

"What's been going on fellas", I said. "What's with the green do?"

"You didn't tell us the hairdos weren't chlorine resistant", the head boy yelped, sounding like a stuck puppy. "We put our heads under in the hotel spa and look at the results!! You didn't warn us. We're suing! Your arse is grass lady. We can't do our gig tonight with this hideous green hair."

Defensively, I grabbed my purse, clutching it tight.

"Don't blame me for your own stupidity. Everyone knows not to put their head under in a spa."

They looked at each other with vacancy in their eyes.

"You're gonna live to regret this lady. Nobody crosses swords with Dicks Forever! and gets away with it!!"

He was turning red in the face and spat as he spoke. They huffed of down the street and I was left alone outside my hairdressing parlour.

The final nail in the coffin was when I did a lady called Stella – she was the mayor's wife. She came in wanting a subtle change and went out with hair the colour of Big Bird. Didn't do much for business. Snobby cow she must have told everybody in town because I went out of business after that. I poured my leftover peroxide into an old Absolut vodka bottle and took it home.

The Laundromat

Just because my hairdressing career was over didn't mean I couldn't excel at something else. I didn't sit around feeling sorry for myself, didn't cry, didn't mope. Sure I got money from my Dad but I still wanted to join the workforce. I wanted to get out and meet people. I pulled myself up by my own bra straps. I got the local paper and looked in the Situations Vacant. I set my sights high. Luckily for me, the local laundromat was hiring. Senior Supervisor. I liked the ring of it. Maybe they would give me a shiny badge to wear on my chest.

I went along the following Monday to meet Beryl the boss of the Laundromat. She was wearing a velour tracksuit that showed off her mono bossom to full effect. She looked to be in her early sixities and was wearing immaculate full makeup – orange lipstick and blue eyeshadow.

"It's a very important role," said Beryl "You can start immediately. We need someone focused and efficient, people need their laundry clean and tidy and not mixed up, people don't want their jock straps tangled up with their hankies. We pay top dollar – ten cents more than minimum wage so we therefore expect our workers to comply with certain standards. Presentation is key. Some girls let themselves go to seed after a while. I want you coming to work proud and pretty."

Beryl gestured towards the stack of magazines, "These will keep you occupied, but don't forget the customers. Remember the customer always comes first, and don't be getting too full of yourself either. It's a powerful position but don't let it go to your head, the last girl we had to fire because she started interrupting peoples spin cycles, pushing buttons willy nilly. I've been a slave to this place for 35 years, you don't need a husband when you work here - I'm married to the laundromat, may as well have a ring upon my finger."

Beryl had a crush on Donald Trump – pictures of him were plastered on the walls of her office; Donald in his swimming pool wearing only his Speedos, Donald in the Oval Office looking authoritative, Donald lying on his bed on his stomach with his chin in his hands and his feet kicked up towards his bum like a Playboy bunny. There was also a picture of the famous man on her coffee mug. She introduced me to one of my special duties which was to pick the tissue fluff off clothing after it had been through the washing machine. A tedious job but I did my best at it – I wanted to impress her. She pulled out two of the washing machines and told me it was my job to clean down the back of them. It looked like it hadn't been cleaned in years. There were dead mice and lint, old tennis shoes and hankies down there - dead cockroaches too.

Second day on the job Beryl was with me supervising. A radio played quietly in the background. I was picking lint off a cardy when I just happened to hear the announcer say 'And now it's time for Dicks Forever! with their new hit single Back Door Boy."

"Hey", I said to Beryl. "Hey I did their hair! Turn it up a bit Beryl."

I didn't want to miss being attached to greatness if DF were going to get their fifteen minutes.

Beryl scowled but did as she was asked. The music played and then it was time for an interview.

"We're here today with Benjamin Foolscap the lead singer of Dicks Forever! Benjamin would you tell us a little about the origins of your song Back Door Boy."

"Sure. It's about one time when I came home drunk and my dad wouldn't let me in through the front door so I had to go round the back."

"Okay. And who arranges venues for you to play in Benjamin or Benny. May I call you Benny?"

"Yes, please do. O Daddy's very well connected. He arranges all our gigs. In fact most of the time he pays the pubs and clubs to take us. But I understand that's normal."

"I see. And that's an intriguing name – Dicks Forever! Could you tell our eager listeners a little about how you came up with the name of your band."

"Well, I feel that women have had their time in the sun. Feminism has run rampant. What about poor old men. We've been overrun. Women have taken over – in the boardroom and in the bedroom. We've had The Vagina Monologues. It's time for the penis to have some power!"

"Thanks for that. Did you hear that listeners? It's time for the penis to have some power. That was Benjamin Foolscap from Dicks Forever! enlightening us with his views. Thank you Benjamin."

Beryl tut-tutted something about *what is the world coming to* and turned down the radio. She said she wanted to leave early so she gave me the keys to lock up, said it was a big responsibility but that she was trusting me.

I was leaving work that evening and was just turning the key in the lock, when somebody came up from behind and put a plastic garbage bag over my head, shoved both arms up behind my back and marched me over to a van that was waiting for me. I was roughly shoved up and into the van and then we sped off through the night. Kidnapped!

Revenge on Tiff

I couldn't breathe properly with a garbage sack over my head. I knew that my assailants would be dangerous - armed most likely. There was a possibility they could be terrorists. So I didn't want to make a fuss.

"Hello," I said. "Could you please remove this garbage sack from over my head?"

I spoke as politely as I could so that I didn't provoke them into killing me.

"We don't want you knowing our identity", one of them growled back. "This is a secret mission. Top secret. We don't want you blabbing to the cops after the event."

"What about just using a blindfold then?", I suggested diplomatically.

They muttered amongst themselves for a bit – it sounded like there were at least four of them, then one of them spoke up.

"Alright then. But you're not to peek while we're taking the garbage sack off."

I promised not to peek.

"What are we gonna use as a blindfold?" I heard one of them ask.

"What about that old T-shirt", another suggested.

Yuk, I didn't want an old sweaty t-shirt wrapped round my lovely hair and face, but I said nothing in case they shot me. One of them removed the garbage sack – I peeked.

"You!" I said. "You!! How dare you!"

It was the boy band. Along with the model whose hair I had peroxided. The lead singer was driving the van.

"It's high time Tiff got a taste of her own medicine don't you think boys", said the lead singer.

They all cheered. My heart sank. They didn't bother with the blindfold now that I knew their identities. What was

I in for? Bloody Sammy! If only I had stuck with my eighties perms, none of this would be happening. It was like a bad dream, a dream I couldn't wake up from.

We drove for what seemed like miles then parked up on a common somewhere. I was petrified. What were they going to do to me?

"Alright then, out you get", said one of them roughly.

I stepped gingerly down from the van, careful not to catch my heels and go for a skate. The last thing I wanted to do was sprain an ankle.

They grabbed my arm and marched me over to the picnic table, "Steady on," I said, I was getting worried now and longed for the safety of the van. They sat me down on the bench and tied my arms behind my back with rope, then looped the rope over my legs and around the bench twice so I couldn't run away.

"Shit just got real sweetheart," one of them said as they started to cut my hair.

"My hair!" I shrieked. "My wonderful hair!"

It had taken me five years to grow it so long. I used top of the range expensive shampoo to keep it sleek and glossy. All gone to waste in seconds, with just a few snips of the scissors. Barbarians. They sniped and they scissored and the hair kept falling. I felt like crying but I didn't want to appear a sook. When they were done they got out the gel and hairspray and began piling in up on top into one big spike. Oh God they were giving me a mohawk. Not content with that – one of them let fire with a can of bright pink spray paint; wind drift brought molecules of it back onto my good clothes. I was distraught – but furious too – how dare they! Who did they think they were to be messing with Tiff's do?

"You'll pay for this", I screeched, when they were done. "Don't think you'll get away with it. O no this is war now."

74

The model laughed vacuously. I noticed that it was her that clutched the spray paint.

"Take me home", I demanded. "Take me home to 82 Bletchley Crescent right now or...or I'm calling the authorities. You've had your fun, I wanna go home."

I reached for my phone. That got them springing into action. I don't think they wanted to tangle with law enforcement. They untied me and scrambled for the van.

"We'll take you home", promised the lead singer. "Just don't call the cops. It was just a bit of fun. We didn't think you'd mind."

"Just get behind the wheel and get driving, dumbo", I demanded. "I've had enough for one evening. I need to be at work at 8am pronto tomorrow to let Beryl in."

They dropped me home. The van ride home was mostly silent. Every now and then the model would let out a vacuous giggle.

I let myself into the house. Looked in the hallway mirror. As expected, a bright pink mohawk jutted up proudly from the top of my head. I looked like a rooster. How was I going to face the world looking like this!?

The Mohawk

At first I was distraught that my eighties perm had been replaced by a sharp, jagged mohawk, but I soon learned to embrace my new do. I went with the flow. The first person to pass comment was of course Beryl. I was cleaning in behind the dryers when she came in to work.

"Now hang on a minute", she said when she saw me. "There's something different about you. Have you lost weight? Got makeup on for a change? No? Oh, I no, oh golly it's *the hair*."

Her hands flew up to her face.

"Where did you get *that* done?"

"It was done *to* me. At a picnic table. On a common. Somewhere on the outskirts of London. Not sure where."

"Well I'm sorry love, but we can't have you coming into work looking like that. What'll the customers think? I'm going to have to let you go."

"But I only just started here."

I tossed her the keys to the shop.

"I know love, but I didn't realise you were going to fix your hair all funny like that or I wouldn't have hired you in the first place. You can't go changing your appearance so drastically and hope to keep your job."

"Fine then," I said. "You can stick your crappy job. I'm sick of the dead mice anyway."

"No need to be like that dear. If you can get your old hair back we can see what we can do."

"I *can't* get my old hair back, can I, you old trout. It's been chopped off."

I grabbed my jacket and handbag and stormed from the laundromat in a huff.

I was marching furiously down the high street, not watching where I was going when I bumped bang smack into Philip. His camera was slung on a strap around his neck – he looked to be in his early forties.

"Love the hairdo", he said. "Bold, confident. It says 'I am me, deal with it world.'"

I looked up, gazed into his baby blues and echoed quietly 'I am me, deal with it world."

I was flattered by the attention of an older man.

"Say, can I take your photo?" he asked. "Against that wall over there. All you have to do is pout a bit and put your hands back against the wall, fingers splayed."

"Sure", I said, flattered.

This was the first time a complete stranger had asked for my photograph.

I did as instructed. Moved back against the wall and gave my best pout and splayed my fingers and Philip clicked away and seemed happy. He invited me out for a drink and I didn't say no. We sat together in the Dog and Duck, me sipping Chardonnay and him drinking beer with a nice frothy head.

"So what do you do for a living?" he asked me.

"Long story. I used to be a hairdresser, but I had a little….incident with the peroxide. Some idiots took exception to what I was doing and put me out of business. So I took a job at the laundromat. Got the sack this morning because of my new hairdo. So I guess I am officially unemployed though I haven't signed on yet. I intend to look for other work."

I clenched my fists.

"I won't be defeated that easily. There's life in the old girl yet."

Philip put his arm around my shoulders.

"That's my girl. How about another Chardonnay to drown your sorrows? Sounds like you've had a rough time of it lately. You're very special. You're unique."

I nodded my head. Downed the new drink in a couple of gulps. It was only 10:30am and I'd skipped breakfast so I was feeling a little tipsy. I put my hand on Philip's knee and began stroking. Then I moved my hand a little higher up his thigh. I was pleased to note that Philip was happy to make my acquaintance. I snuggled in closer and put my head upon his chest. I could hear his heart thumping. Philips skulled the rest of his beer and said "how about we go back to my place" in a deep manly voice.

How could a girl resist? I don't want anybody thinking I am a tart. I don't do this kind of thing often. Enough. Philip drove a red sports car with a sun roof. He put on a pair of wraparound sunglasses and put the top down and we drove through the Peckham streets feeling like King and Queen of the universe. I waved out the windows and called out 'yoo-hoo' to several passersby.

We arrived in Brixton at Philip's pad. We went in through the front door and into the living room. Philip bought me another glass of white wine and took a Budweiser for himself, then brought out a bag of white powder and put it down upon the table.

"What this?" I asked. "Icing sugar?"

I put my finger in and licked it. My gums tingled and then went numb.

"Funny tasting icing sugar", I said. "Bet your Mum didn't give you that."

I winked at him. One thing led to another and we were in flagrante delicito, doing it doggy style facing the TV. We had been going for about ten minutes and we must not have heard the front door open or shut. The next thing I knew one of Philip's flatmates was standing in the doorway, mouth open.

"O Philip", he said. "I've just finished a hard shift at the club. I don't want to come home and see this. You could at least have gone to the bedroom."

Philip rolled away and grabbed for the TV remote.

"We were just watching *Hymns of Praise* on TV", he said, cranking up the volume.

"Yeah right. Come on. Take it to the bedroom. I need to use the dining area, I have to cook some brunch and I don't want to see you two bunny rabbits going at it."

The mood was ruined. Philip said we should go watch the kites at Brockwell Park. I giggled and said okay. We trotted down the road to the park and sat on the side of the common watching the multi-coloured shapes swing and sway in the breeze – we were as high as kites ourselves. After a couple of hours the booze and coke started to wear off and I asked Philip to take me home.

"I'll cherish these lovely memories we've made", I said, kicking one heel up behind me.

Philip took me back to the car. I figured he was safe to drive by now. We roared through the London streets back to my place. I thought about asking him in but I didn't want him to think I was too easy. I gave him a peck on the cheek and went to say goodnight but then realized it was only mid-afternoon.

"Good afternoon", I said with a giggle and skipped merrily up the stairs.

What a day. If only stuffy old Beryl knew what I had been up to!

Philip

Philip and I became joined at the hip. I didn't mind that he was twice my age – in fact, I liked it. He was worldly wise, he could teach me the ways of the world. However, the first time I entered his bedroom I did notice that the walls were plastered with pictures of young women – women in their late teen and early twenties and I did wonder why.

"How come you've got all these pictures of women around?" I asked. "Where's my picture?"

I pouted.

"I thought I was special and unique."

"All these girls were special and unique," said Philip in his deep manly voice, the voice I could not resist.

He put his arm around my shoulders. "Come on sweetheart. I promise to put up a photo of you. You can perch between Stella and Sheryl. They thought they were special and unique too."

I didn't like being 'perched' between Stella and Sheryl much, I wanted a whole wall to myself but I put up with it because I was so keen on Philip.

I had been seeing Philip for about four months when Sammy appeared to me in a vision. I was washing my dishes at the kitchen sink when he descended in a cloud of gold glitter.

O Sammy, I thought. *How tacky. Surely you can do better than gold glitter.*

"Who's the other man you've been galavanting round the town with then?", Sammy demanded.

"He's not a patch on me. Doesn't even own a Harley. What's with that tacky red sports car?"

I couldn't believe it. Sammy was jealous.

"Oh, come on Sammy", I said. "Play the game. You've been dead for over a year and a woman has...needs. You're free to sew your wild oats. Don't they have women in the afterlife?"

"None that I fancy. There's a headless horsewoman up here and I've seen Joan of Arc strutting her stuff down heaven's main thoroughfare but none of them are you babe. Can't you just wait till you die and then we can be together for all eternity?"

"O Sammy get a grip. I can't go without....love...for decades. Can't you understand that?"

"I guess I'll just have to come to terms with it", he replied sulkily. "Just remember though – I can see everything from my vantage point and I don't like seeing you in the sack with that....that...loser. He's a right sleaze. What's with all those pictures of other women on the bedroom wall?"

"They were just friends", I said quickly.

"Yeah right. *Special and unique.* God, what a line."

And with that the vision began to crackle and fade, like an untuned TV set, till it disappeared completely.

I didn't bother to find other work. I just lived off the money my Dad sent each month. Philip was overly fond of the white powder. He spend a fortune on it. I just dabbled. I worried that he would lose his septum and look like Daniella Westbrook. One summer evening we were together at his place after having a few drinks, when he bought out not just one but two bags of the stuff. I gasped. "Philip", I said. "Are you sure? There's just the two of us. I can't do a bag on my own – how much are *you* going to do?"

He shrugged.

"Enough", he said glibly.

I giggled and rolled up a ten pound bill. Snorted some of the 'icing sugar'. Started buzzing.

Well, God only knows what happened after that, but the next thing I knew one of the bags was empty and Philip was rolling on the floor, clutching his chest and groaning. "Quick babe, quick, call an ambulance. No wait. They'll know we've been doing cocaine. You drive me – you *can* drive can't you?"

I nodded. I'd had a couple of driving lessons out in Essex once when I was fifteen.

I thought quickly. I hauled Philip to his feet and put his arm around my shoulders, then half-dragged him down to the street. The red sports car was parked up against the curb. I positioned Philip in the passenger seat, then hopped round to the driver's side. Started the engine. Vrooom. We were off. I had been given driving lessons in an automatic and this was a manual so we bunny-hopped a bit but Philip was in too much pain to notice, groaning and clutching his chest and carrying on. We didn't have a map but Philip had a GPS system so I programmed in King's College Hospital, which was the hospital my Nan died at. The GPS system started narrating – 'Dalberg Rd 200 metres turn right'. I bunny-hopped a bit. I breathed deeply into both nostrils. I obeyed. I turned right. 'Barnwell Rd 500 metres, turn left'. I turned left into Barnwell. This was a breeze. If only Philip would shut up he was disturbing my concentration. 'Railton Road, 200 metres, turn right'. I was falling in love with the GPS. It made things so easy. If only life had a GPS, telling you what direction to take when you became unsure.

We made it to the hospital. I got out of the car and gave myself a big pat on the back and said 'Well done Tiff!' There was just a small amount of paint removed from the side of the car from where I had side-swiped another vehicle but nobody had noticed. We walked through into A&E and I sat Philip down in a hard plastic chair. I walked up to the counter. The nurse was on the phone.

"No Timothy", she was saying. "You leave the microwave popcorn *in* the bag. You need to cook it for at least 10 minutes or it won't be done properly. Alright. Don't break anything while Mummy's at work."

She hung up and shot me a cold look.

"How can I help?"

"My boyfriend's having a heart attack."

The phone rang again. The nurse picked up the phone.

"No Timothy the saveloys stay in the water for at least fifteen minutes until they start falling apart. I got you three big bags of crisps to keep you happy - they are on the bottom shelf of the pantry. There's always the toastie pie maker if you're still hungry."

I stomped my white tasseled high heeled boot upon the floor.

"Excuse me lady", I said. "A man's life is in danger here and you're on the phone chatting to your son about saveloys. Don't you think you should get your priorities straight?"

The nurse put down the phone.

"We'll get to you in a minute. You're not the only one waiting. Can't you see A&E is full of casualties. What make you think you're special and unique. We see heart attacks every day – most people live through it."

I needed something to calm my shattered nerves.

"Could I have a cup of chamomile tea please?" I asked a nurse who was walking by.

"This is the NHS love it's gumboot or nothing," came the gruff answer.

Philip clutched his chest.

"I'm dying here."

"Then die quietly", snapped one of the friendlier nurses.

I looked over at the nursing station. Through the glass I could see that two of the nurses were checking their Facebook accounts while one of the male nurses appeared to be looking at a porn magazine. I rapped on the glass near the male.

"Hello", I said. "I know you might find XXX hot sex bunnies very engrossing but my boyfriend is having a heart attack could you please help us."

He put down his magazine, looking flustered and guilty.

"Alright sweetheart, keep yer knickers on. Everybody round here needs help. I'm sure somebody will get to him in a minute."

He went back to his magazine, flicking a page as he did so.

I breathed a heavy sigh and got us both a drink from the water cooler.

"Christ", I said. "What do you have to do to get some assistance round here?"

Philip fell to the floor. His lips were turning blue and his eyes were rolling back in his head. He was gasping for breath.

"Quick", I said. "Somebody get that vibrating machine thingy."

Finally, somebody came across with a big machine, unbuttoned Philip's shirt and put some sticky pads on his chest, obeying the voice prompts. They began pushing buttons at random and Philip twitched violently upon the floor. My God – they were electrocuting him! The nurses started arguing amongst themselves about how to use the machine. They pushed some buttons again and sparks flew out the sides of the pads on Philip's chest. He spasmed and was still. I raced to his side and checked his pulse. Nothing. I took my makeup mirror out of my handbag and checked for his breath. Nothing. Philip was as dead as a dodo. Electrocuted by A&E staff.

I burst into tears.

"This is appalling", I sobbed. "You've murdered Philip. He was a lovely man, wouldn't harm a fly. I want to talk to management. Heads must roll. Somebody must be held accountable."

One of the nurses trotted away and came back with the head doctor.

"Hi I'm Trevor", he said, looking me up and down. "What seems to be the problem?"

"My boyfriend is dead", I said. "He came in here having a heart attack and nobody attended to him on time."

"Oh dear", he said, staring at my boobs. "Dead you say. That's no good. Why don't I take your number and I can investigate and let you know the results of the case."

He winked.

I took a pen and paper out of my handbag and gave him my number, flattered by the attention. Satisfied that all had been resolved, I made my way back to the sports car and drove home, hoping that Philip hadn't made a will so that I would be able to keep the car.

The Doctor

It took a lot of time and effort to keep the mohawk looking ship-shape. I used special hair products on it and had already re-spray painted it pink twice as the colour had started to dim and fade. I always liked to take pride in my appearance.

A week after Philip had died my phone rang. It was the doctor, wanting to know what I was doing on Saturday night.

"I've got a funeral to attend", I said.

"What are you doing afterwards?"

"I've got the after party to go to", I said. "Lots of free booze."

"Are you trying to tempt me?"

"Come along if you like. More the merrier. Hopefully I'll have something to celebrate 'cause they will have read the will."

Philip's parents organized the funeral. They saw me eyeing up the red sports car and subtly let me know that it was going up for sale, proceeds heading towards their pocket. I wore a bright red skin tight strapless dress to the funeral – it was Philip's favourite dress on me. His parents gave me sideways looks but I didn't mind. It was an open coffin, the dude on the microphone said a few words and then asked if anybody wanted to come and put a flower on the body. A great long queue of women, I counted 25, lined up to place their flowers. All the women looked about my age. The second to last woman spent forever gazing into the coffin, her shoulders heaving with sobs. An uncomfortable silence fell over the crowd. After five minutes of sobbing, she attempted to throw herself into the coffin with Philip and had to be detained and escorted off by security. I was shocked; it was as if *she* was his current girlfriend. Maybe she was – it wouldn't have surprised me if Philip was cheating on me all along.

The will was read out. He everything except the car to Stella and Sheryl – blonde twins who looked like they'd stepped out of a Sweet Valley High book. The car he left to me. I saw his parents spit tacks. Somebody threw a chocolate éclair at Stella when the will was announced and it hit her in the side of the head. A minor brawl broke out. I couldn't believe that Philip had left me nothing in the will, so I walked off; tears were welling in my eyes.

I ran bang smack into Trevor the doctor. A lit cigarette dangled between his fingers.
"Hey babe" he said. "Where you going in such a hurry?"
"A fight broke out", I said.
He glanced over at the brawl.
"Wow. Chaos reigns. You wanna drink?"
I nodded. I needed something to help me get through. We walked the short distance to where the after party was being held – in the same building as the funeral – just down the corridor and to the right.
"Gin please", I said.
He nodded briskly then headed for the bar, puffing furiously on his cigarette as if his life depended on it.

We sat down together in one of the booths and Trevor lit one cigarette from the end of another. *What class!*, I thought. I could tell he was a man of distinction and style. He was drinking a funny coloured liqueur. I asked him what it was.
"Absinth", he answered.
"Have you had a good week?" I asked.
"Not really. Lost two patients."
He didn't elaborate so I didn't ask for details.

I sipped my gin, eyeing up Trevor as I did so and I saw him trying to look down the front of my dress. I was flattered by the attention. We drank on, into the evening, until the faces of the other funeral attendees began to blur. Trevor took my hand. I didn't resist. I saw Philip's parents giving me looks of disapproval and felt a slight twinge of guilt, but the alcohol dulled it. Anyway, he hadn't left me anything in the will and he was dead now, so he wouldn't have a clue about what was going on. Trevor invited me back to his house. He chainsmoked all the way through the intercourse, dropping hot ash on me. I was very disappointed in this and told him he had a nicotine addiction problem and should try patches or the gum.

"Hey so what else is news", he said glibly, lighting another fag.

In the morning he was quite the gentleman and made me coffee and eggs benedict. I was watching my figure so I only had half the breakfast and left the other half congealing on the plate. Trevor was paged and had to go to work hungover. It was a heart attack he was meant to be tending to, but he took his sweet time, tending to me first and making sure I was okay and could get home safely. He asked me to meet him for lunch the next day and I agreed.

I showed up at the hospital where Trevor worked wearing a sparkly gold top with thin spaghetti straps and my best leather mini, teamed with pink heels to match my mohawk.

As I entered the hospital café where we had arranged to meet I scanned the room looking expectantly for Trevor. I couldn't believe I was dating a doctor my luck was changing, I'd be set for life.

I didn't see him straight away, so I sat down at the nearest two seater table. Just as I sat down I heard vacuous giggles from the corner. I looked over to see Trevor sitting with a group of nurses- there must have been about four or five all gazing at Trevor attentively, giggling at his every word. I felt a wave of jealousy. Without thinking I marched over.

"Excuse me"' I screeched, "When does our lunch date start?"

The doctor turned to face me.

"Sorry" he said. "I didn't see you sitting over there. I was just entertaining these lovely ladies."

"Yes, looks like it", I snapped.

"Would you like to join us."

"No I want to have lunch with you alone."

"Oh, getting possessive are we? What is it – second date?" teased one of the nurses.

I shot the nurse a cold look, turned on my pink heels and marched back to the table, hoping that Trevor would follow.

He stayed talking with the nurses for a further five minutes and I was just about to leave when he came sauntering over.

"So what do you fancy for lunch then?"

"Are you sure you can spare me the time", I replied coldly. "Don't bust your boiler."

"Oh come on sweetheart they're just my work colleagues. We were just having a team meeting." He paused. "Did you know you're really beautiful when you're angry."

"Don't try that old line on me. I know your type. Man about town. Ladies man. Well, I'm too jaded for you to be breaking my heart. I've been around the town too you know."

"Have you now. I never would have picked it. How about we skip lunch and I'll show you the linen room?"

"The linen room! Is that where they do it in hospitals. I always did wonder."

"No it's just that I think I left my belt in there."

"Oh okay then." I said quickly. "I can help you find it."

We got up and I followed him dutifully down the corridor, we passed a group of what appeared to be student nurses, they giggled when they saw Trevor.

"Hi Doctor Trevor" they chorused in flirty unison.

We arrived at the Linen room, Trevor locked the door and looked at me with a seducing glance.

"Hey I thought we were just here to find your belt", I said

Trevor suddenly got a strange look on his face and went as white as the sheets he was standing next to. Before I knew it he dropped to the floor, twitched a little and stopped moving.

"Trevor! I exclaimed "What are you doing, this isn't funny you are scaring me".

He didn't answer - I ran out to the corridor and pushed the emergency call button. That's the last thing I remembered as I dropped to the floor myself in a faint.

When I came to I was lying in a hospital bed- a nurse was standing near me, "Trevor?" I said

She turned and looked at me, "Sorry love, Doctor Trevor had an aneurysm" then added sarcastically "When you two were counting the linen, he died".

My vision narrowed, my last thoughts were, *not again!* then I lost consciousness for the second time.

It turns out that Trevor's aneurysm was most likely caused by his 50 a day smoking habit. So I found myself the following Tuesday attending yet another funeral. When they read Trevor's will I found that he had left me absolutely nothing.

After the funeral I went home to drown my sorrows. This was the third man that had died on me. I poured myself a vodka and lemonade, skulled it back, then poured another. I went through into the bathroom to find some Valium. I took six Valium and found sitting on the edge of the bath a bottle of Absolut Vodka that was a quarter full. Score! All I wanted was to write myself off. I could not handle being a black widow. I took the Absolut through into the kitchen and mixed it with some lemonade. Knocked it back. It tasted a bit funny but I kept it down. I poured myself another vodka and lemonade. By now I was feeling pleasantly smashed although there was a bit of a burning sensation in my throat. I dismissed this feeling and finished off the vodka I had found in the bathroom.

I went to the bedroom to lie down. It was then I remembered the peroxide I had stashed in the vodka bottle. O God I was going to die! It was going to be curtains for Tiff!

The visions started. Dying wasn't so bad. Sammy didn't let me down – he came for me in a horse-drawn golden chariot, surrounded by angels with peroxided hair, showered in gold glitter.

"Don't worry babe. I'm here to take you to heaven. It's nice up there. Time to leave your earthly body behind and ascend."

I stepped out of my body. My spirit climbed into the chariot next to Sammy and the horses began to pull us skywards, galloping through the sky. As I looked down I could see planet earth underneath me, growing smaller and smaller as we headed towards heaven, my problems fading away and becoming more and more insignificant. I was pure spirit now, an angel or a goddess, one of the immortals. As we went through the Pearly Gates St Pete doffed his hat to me and said 'Welcome home lass' and winked. The streets of heaven were lined with gold and pearls and shined beautifully. I had never been anywhere so glorious and I was glad that I had died and gone to heaven. The first people I saw were Trevor and Philip, sitting on silver thrones and beckoning me to go over and talk. I didn't want to make Sammy jealous. After all, he was my first true love, so I did not approach these other men. Instead Sammy and I continued our tour through the streets, finishing up at a lovely palace with four turrets and a flag flying outside. All my dreams had been realized in the afterlife.

FRESH WOLVES

It started with just the first wolf. I met him in the forest walking home from Granny's place. I sensed something stalking me, so I turned around and faced him. He paused for an instant. I took out the gun I had stashed in my knickers and shot him right between the eyes. He keeled over, dead. I picked him up by the forepaws and slung him over my back. Blood dripped down between my shoulder blades. Mother yelped when she saw him.

"Yikes, what've you got there?" she asked.

I played it nonchalant.

"Oh, just an old wolf," I replied.

"Quick," she said. "Bring him inside the cabin before the other wolves see and start plotting revenge."

I lugged the wolf inside and plopped him down upon the cabin floor. Mother took out her biggest stewing pot from under the stove and handed me Father's hunting knife.

"Quick," she said. "Get skinning."

I set to with the knife, scraping away the wolf's skin and then gutting him. The fresh stench of entrails assaulted my nostrils. I cut steaks from the fore and hind quarters and handed them to Mother who chopped them into smaller portions for the cooking pot. Mother took carrots, leeks and potatoes from the cupboard and added them to the stew.

"This'll be delicious," she said. "Your father'll be rapt."

For the next two months, I did a wolf a week. I started plumping up, my buttocks ballooning, my stomach hanging out above the belt of my jeans. I'd never been so content, so well fed. But then the cravings started. One wolf a week just wasn't enough. *More, more, more* cried my stomach, my greed. I started doing two, then three wolves a week. It was sometime in June when the ghosts began visiting. I was lying in bed, reading *Wuthering Heights,* when I heard a scratching at the windowpane. I rose from my bed and drew back the curtains. Ghostly grey wolf-shaped forms with piercing red eyes hovered on the other side of the pane, dragging their claws down the glass. Wolf incubi! I screamed and called for Mother. She came running, candle in hand.

"Quick," she cried. "Get the special gun from the mantelpiece. The one with the silver bullets. The one that Father keeps for best."

I ran for the gun and headed back to the bedroom. Mother took the weapon from my hands and shot at the wolves through the glass. To no avail. These were not werewolves, but wolf ghosts – you cannot kill the dead. The glass no longer held them. One of them came through the pane and inhabited me. I looked in the mirror and howled, examining my fangs, my paws, my haunted and hungry red eyes.

THE RISING EPIDEMIC OF BULLYING

We live in enlightened, feminist, non-racist, non-sexist times – or so we are told. So we are taught to believe. *Girls can do anything*: so the slogan ran when I was a girl. And so the picture of *Keisha* Castle-Hughes riding on the back of a water-bound mammal would have us believe.

I grew up in a kind, caring, loving household. There were boundaries, of course, but they weren't too draconian. I was raised to believe that I could achieve my goals: I could put a marker-post down in the future, head towards it with conviction and vigour and, all things being equal, I could reach my goal. I could compete with the men – and with other women. I could be a go-getter, an achiever, a winner. If not Numero Uno, then perhaps Numero Novantanove. My parents tried to teach me strategies that I could use to protect myself. When I was bullied while cleaning a fish factory – 'you've missed a fish scale'; 'look me in the eye when I'm trying to bully you' – my parents told me to complain to the manager. The bully promptly pulled her head in and I was given a glowing reference stating that I had great 'strength of character'.

I progressed to university, a nice middle-class girl doing a B.A./LLB – inoffensive enough, and yet people seemed determined to treat me as somehow other; different.

When I was taken home to meet the parents of my first boyfriend the quizzing began.

"So what kind of contraception are you on?" asked his father.

"Um, I'm sort of on the pill," I tentatively replied. "Sort of? Are you or aren't you?," he shot back.

"I am."

"Good. Because the next thing you know I won't be supporting just you and Richard, I'll be supporting thirty-three kids as well."

At the age I am now, thirty-eight, with no children at all, I find myself wondering what I did to deserve such treatment. Perhaps being born female was enough. *Born this way,* as Lady Gaga would say. How could I have understood, when I came sliding forth from my mother's womb, that my gender would prove to be so constricting? My parents created a safe place, a shelter. I was protected from many of the world's evils. I was taught to play nice. I wasn't warned about all the people rolling crooked dice. The wolves and the jackals. Little did I realize how riddled the world is with corruption and vice; with envy, with spite, with *foul play.*

When my first novel came out I hadn't expected such a furore. Sure, I was only young, but did people really have to get so up in arms about it? I found myself in the middle of a bizarre process of simultaneous deification and vilification. This wasn't what I had wanted. I had wanted to publish under a pseudonym, but it had been written into my contract that I had to use my own name. I had to put up with public humiliation, pack hatred, people sneering at me in the street.

"Why don't I tell you to just fuck off then!" yelled an announcer at Radio New Zealand after I baulked at reading a passage from my novel aloud.

"Suicide's good for sales", said my editor's husband.

"What makes you think anybody wants to know what's going on in your head?" asked my father.

"Today's news, tomorrow's fish and chips", chimed in my friend's Dad.

Still, it could have been worse. Some writers get death threats. I seemed to attract a sort of morbid curiosity, like a weird lab specimen that somebody had captured to keep in a jar for public display. People seemed more interested in me than the book. I came to realize that (O, how Plath-like) there would have to be two of me; the public self and the private one. The more that other people are trying to invade your privacy, the thicker must be the wall that keeps them out. I, for one, had no desire to end up as tabloid fodder, a literary Middleton, preyed on by *paparazzi.*

There were role models but they were few and far between. There were examples of people who had won despite, or perhaps because of, obstacles. There was Kristen Hersh, who started up her band in her early teens when some form of mental illness started making its shock waves felt. My schoolmate Cindy Mosey lost her entire family in a plane crash of which she was the sole survivor, and yet she went on to become three-times world kite surf champion. She was a good example of somebody who had lost everything and then gone on to win. All I can tell you about being female is this: *Any time I was good at something I got harassed.* So, why bother? Surely it's better just to lie low and sit around the house, smoking pot and watching *Dogs With Jobs* on the telly all day. Maybe I really am an obsessive over-achiever. More likely, I'm of the personality type that has to have something to do. Also, once I learn how to do something, I am quickly bored by it. For me, the fun is in the learning. When I moved to London in 1998, I felt as if I was engaged in a complicated game of chess. All I had to my name were my two novels, my honours degree in English Literature and two thousand pounds that I had saved while fruit picking. I wondered what would become of me. My anxieties and doubts circled my head like tortured flies. How would I find the time to pen my tomes? How would I support myself? How would I survive? How would I find my way in the world? I was playing straight, but everyone around me was crooked. I felt as if somebody had set me down at a chessboard and told me to play my game, while all around me other people were performing their own very complicated manoeuvres. Or maybe it was the other way round. Maybe *I* was crooked and they were straight. The city was a jungle. Games were being played. And what sort of chess piece was I? A queen, a pawn, or something mid-range, a rook or knight perhaps? The female sales executives in the fund management firm where I worked seemed pathologically competitive with each other. One would even delete the other's emails from the boss's inbox, so that he wouldn't be able to credit her with the work she'd done. What was to stop me from becoming like the people around me? What was to stop *me* from becoming an exploiter, a bully, a crook? Conscience, I think. Morals – if I still had any. But why *should* I be nice? Why should I be *good*? Maybe being a bitch would get me further. Maybe I could turn into a bully to deter other people from bullying me. Maybe I should just ditch whatever morals I had and turn into a complete crim. Start dealing coke and whizz, stealing cars, maybe turning tricks in a brothel.

So, what do you know about Fund Management? I was asked by an older gentleman at the interview for a P.A position.

Not a lot, but maybe you could tell me something about it, I responded.

Oh, I hate people who throw the question back at you, was the reply.

The British version of bullying is to try and make a person feel ganged-up on, out-numbered, mobbed. When I was made redundant from my Fund Management job, I was called into an office where a number of my colleagues were gathered around a table in a manner designed to intimidate. They were all on one side of the table, sitting up, backs straight, all very formal, like the judges on *The X Factor* or *Dragon's Den*, while I, a lone ranger, was on the other side. Perhaps, I thought, they are hoping for me to audition for a different role – *Flashdance* style. No matter how polite I was, no matter how humble, no matter how *sweet*, I still had to put up with being vilified. I've endured being physically hit at work, not by a man, but by a woman – '*Helena Carr, Senior Sales Executive.*'

There I am, a good little Kiwi, working God only knows how many hours per week, not bothering anybody, and along she comes, to cuff the back of my head.

Belt.

Don't touch my head.

Belt.

Don't (*pause*) touch (*pause*) my head.

In the end, despite being brought up to be a pacifist, and never having hit another human in my life, I just turned around and belted her back. Shortly afterwards I was made redundant but it was worth it for the satisfaction of whacking her. A writer will take revenge through fiction. Helena told me that *Boxing Helena* was based on her. When she was living in California, a writer, let's call him James, had a crush on her. David Lynch's daughter, Jennifer Lynch, had a crush on the writer. Jennifer observed the relationship between Helena and James and wrote the script for the film *Boxing Helena.* Constantly writing about somebody, or making them your muse, can be a form of appropriation, oppression or 'boxing in'.

Women, far more than men, are made to feel vulnerable and threatened. We are picked on more. We are harassed, put down, patronized, belittled and made to feel small – more often than not by other women, as well as men. Recent research shows that women are 71% more likely to be bullied by another woman, whereas the chances of a woman being bullied by a man are a much lower 46%. Then there's the good old female favourite – ostracism. Bonding through exclusion. The typical teenage trick. What woman hasn't experienced being driven out of a gang of girls? One of the main reasons I got into I.T. was that I thought it would be male-dominated and therefore less bitchy – as it turns out, most of the men were just as catty as the women.

I hate my life. I'm looking for a victim, admitted my last boss as she cruised the office for targets. Is it me, or is workplace bullying becoming endemic? Surely I'm not so much of a nerd, so socially retarded, that I actually invite abuse? Or am I? No, it's not just me. Bullying is on the rise. According to a recent global survey by Monster, 63% of respondents and a massive 83% of Europeans say that they have been the victim of workplace bullying. Why? Personally, I think it's because they're all crammed in together like chickens, frustration oozing from every feather and nobody to peck at apart from the chicken in the next coop over, or more likely and more often, the chicken in the coop underneath. A European corporate chicken is a battery hen; a New Zealand chicken is relatively free range. And yet, workplace bullying is on the rise here too. Maybe when times are tough the sociopaths and psychopaths know they can get away with more nasty behaviour, because people won't risk standing up for themselves in case they lose their jobs.

Bullying can be insidious and sneaky. You can set somebody up to fail by allocating them tasks that they are unable to complete in the given timeframe and then complaining that they didn't complete their work on time. Patronizing somebody is also a form of bullying, since talking down to a person is designed to make them feel small and powerless. Then there is the trick of standing somebody up – saying you are going to be somewhere or do something and failing to deliver. My career counsellor pulled this trick a couple of times. I was as busy as all hell and he kept setting up appointments with me and then forgetting, or failing, to turn up. Helpful behaviour from a career counsellor.

These days, we have cyber-bullying: one kid threatening, humiliating or intimidating another online. This form of bullying is prevalent amongst teenagers. Suicides can result. And bullying is present in academia – my sister's PhD supervisor returned her thesis with HATE IT penned across the top in bright-red ink. We've all heard of male lecturers who mark the women harder than the men. And no matter how much I tell myself, *it's not you, it's them*, I can't help but internalize some of society's misogynistic hatred. By publishing fiction I am, in my uncle's words, 'an ego-tripper.' No matter how truthful I am, I still have to put up with being called a liar. *It's only envy.* Is it?

After three years working as a secretary and personal assistant, I decided to find a profession that would enable me to earn the money to buy the time to write. I settled on Computer Science. It seemed like something I could master if I put my mind to it. I had the curiosity. I wanted to know how it all worked. There weren't too many hurdles and some of the people I studied with were genuinely nice. I was doing fine until my supervisor told me to rewrite my entire Masters thesis three weeks before it was due, on some flimsy pretence such as 'Class Diagrams can't be used with PHP' and then falsely accused me of using foul language. He was Greek. He spelt it *fowl*. Perhaps he'd overheard me clucking in the corridor. It wasn't the end of the world. I swapped supervisors and was given a 'B.'

I joined a posh, blue-chip firm, and was put to work under Ed Simpson, who was clearly one of life's brighter sparks. He'd turned down an offer at NASA to take this job. Ed and I had at least one thing in common – we both wanted to be fighter pilots when we were young. He seemed driven by inner demons, and would work until midnight and beyond. I have fond memories of leaving work at three a.m., drunk with tiredness. Neither of the men I was with had thought ahead to book a hotel or a taxi. I guess they were so wrapped up in solving their own complicated problems that they forgot to arrange transport or accommodation. There was nothing funny going on between us; we were just three exhausted people looking for somewhere to rest. After all, sometimes, clever people do stupid things. My father, who is a retired electrical engineer, nearly electrocuted me after forgetting to turn off the mains while we were installing a lamp.

I've put up with verbal abuse. By various male colleagues I have been called a *bitch, a smart arse, a tart* and *a psycho.* If things were genuinely fair in the gender war, why did I have to put up with *that* bullshit in this day and age? Especially in a company that bleated on about 'inclusion and diversity in the workplace'. I've been followed home from work by fellow Peckhamites. "Hey you! You pretty lady. Why don't you stop and talk to me?" *Um, because you might rape or murder me.*

Sometimes I demonstrated not so much bravery as a sort of naive stupidity. Walking home by myself through Hackney at midnight with my headphones on, listening to British Sea Power, I was almost mugged. I say 'almost' because the mugger seemed to lose interest partway through.

"Gimme your money," he muttered half-heartedly.

I'd just had a lovely holiday in the Greek islands, so I was very relaxed.

"I've only got ten pounds," I said, opening up my purse.

"Oh, forget it then," he said, and wandered off.

Funnily enough, I almost felt cheated. *Aren't I even worth mugging?* I felt like yelling. *Come back here and mug me properly. I'd get on that bus if I were you,* a local black woman shouted out her window.

I've been mugged in a shop. My ex-husband and I were living in Dalston on the edge of Hackney, and I was working full-time and studying in my evenings. I stepped out to buy a pint of milk. Two large men entered the shop. As the shop assistant was ringing up the purchase, one of the men pulled out a gun and shoved it in his face. The other man grabbed me around the shoulders. I squirmed and ran free, went sprinting off down the street, heart thudding. When I returned to the scene to give evidence, the cops didn't want to know.

Beware of thirty-three – so Jarvis Cocker tells us. Perhaps I should have heeded his warnings, for when I hit this age I suffered some sort of drastic cognitive malfunction. I couldn't cope with my double load of I.T. and attempted literature. My mind went blank, or hit a blackout. Call it an early mid-life crisis, call it burn-out, call it an undiagnosed brain tumour starting to make its effects felt – suddenly, I couldn't understand what people were saying to me. Nothing seemed to compute. It seemed as if I was expected to leap through a series of flaming hoops while juggling miscellaneous objects. Most citizens of modern society will know the feeling: we know we're headed for a breakdown when the demands being placed on us by ourselves or others exceed our adult capabilities. My right shoulder seized up with RSI so I went to an acupuncturist. When I told him I was a writer he said, "So do you think you're quite a perceptive person?"

"I guess"

"So if a woman was standing behind you staring at the back of your head would you feel it?"

"I suppose so."

"What if it was the stare of a horny man?"

It was a terrible trick, an invasion of my personal boundaries. I didn't say anything, but for some reason this comment has haunted me ever afterwards. I think it was because it was such a high-end acupuncturist, situated in Harley Street, no less, that it creeped me out so much more than if it had just been the good old Melbourne Grove Medical Centre.

When my father wrote to the doctor at the Melbourne Grove surgery about the acupuncturist, he was told that he was a 'revered figure.' A revered figure who sexually harasses his clients. Great. What was I supposed to learn from all this? That the nice guys finish last? That upper-class British men still think it's all right to sexually harass women just because they are in positions of power and influence? There was the agent who stared at my tits and told me I 'looked marketable.' There was the world-famous poet who made smutty comments to me at a literary prize-giving – something about 'wanting to take all somebody's clothes off and lay them out on the table.' Why, Lord, *why?* Maybe they were trying to intimidate me into not succeeding. Perhaps it was meant to be flattering, but it came across as creepy.

I went on a city ski trip to Italy with some people from the company. A bunch of yobs were getting pissed in the courtyard outside the hotel window. I waited until three in the morning, and then told them to pack it up.

Shut up ya Aussie bitch or I'll come up there and rape ya, one gentleman hollered back.

British chivalry at its finest. He started climbing up the railing. I grabbed the nearest bottle of Veuve and hiffed it out the window at him. It narrowly missed him, but fell to the courtyard below and smashed into a thousand pieces. The following morning, a colleague of one of the yobs came up to me and apologized.

"We wouldn't have bought him along, but he's one of our best skiers. He doesn't have any fear. He just points his skis downhill and goes for it."

103

"That's okay," I said. "I wasn't offended that he called me a bitch; I was miffed that he thought I was from Australia."

Women are patronized. There's the boyfriend who says "Hey, you're really cute when you're angry," (thus invalidating a genuine emotion). There's the friend or acquaintance who comments "Gosh, I just love that dress you have on. So much better than that awful frock you were wearing last week," or "Your hair looks great dyed red. Especially compared to that jet black colour you had last year."

But wait. It gets worse. I slogged my guts out for two years solid and was up for accelerated promotion. A new manager named Richard was rolled onto the project. He saw what a good worker I was and especially asked to have me on his team. I didn't have to ask him a single question and yet Kent, the programmer sitting next to me, continuously asked questions and was still promoted.

"Hey, Laura. In Greece the man beats the woman like an octopus," said Kent one day, slamming his palm down on the desk with quite some force. *Sometimes perceived as difficult* was written on my file.

But what about Richard and *his* managerial skills? Coming into work and shoving his cheque for thirty grand (a gift from some aunt or other) into my face, whilst knowing full well that it would take me ten years to save such a sum. He told me that he'd been kicked out, or rather 'sent down' from Cambridge. He gave me all the work and hogged all the glory.

"So who do you think said you shouldn't be promoted?" he taunted me.

"Evan."

"And?"

"Thomas."

"And?"

"Harry."

"So, what will you do if you don't get promoted?"

Various options flitted through my mind.

Option A: Go postal, shooting myself and taking out a few of my colleagues at the same time.

Option B: Flee for the colonies.

Option C: Jump out the window.

"Leave, I guess," I said.

I wonder now why I played along. I should've told him to stick it and walked out.

"You just don't have any respect for me, do you?" he queried one day.

What did he expect me to do? Bow down and kiss the hem of his Eton-educated garment?

Apparently I wasn't 'mature enough' to have my promotion. And yet I had seen my previous manager, Ed, rant and rave and yell and they still gave him *his* promotion and all I'd had was one little 'girly fit' – a *yap*. *So much wrong with this company,* commented a colleague, and yet nobody could really do anything about it. And now, to be honest, I don't care. I'm in my happy place – working for myself.

On the final project I was on, a third of the people were off sick with stress leave. Most of those left behind despised their lives. The boss started bullying me by telling me to do the wrong things and then laughing at me when I obeyed her instructions. Telling me to fix bugs and then laughing at me when I did it.

"The clue was that nobody else was doing that."

"That's wicked", said her boyfriend, who was on the same project.

Bye, bye. Wave bye bye, he said as I was leaving work.

They started up with the wolf laugh. *Oh hoo hoo.*

What the hell was all this anyway? Some kind of weird mind-game? What are these people getting out of playing these games? A power trip? Are they really that fucked up, that their only fun is attempting to give somebody else a nervous breakdown for blood-sport? *I thought they banned fox-hunting in Britain*, commented a friend when I relayed the incident to her.

My colleagues were workaholics. One senior executive admitted he suffered panic attacks on holiday. Surely that's not normal. Money and status were gods to these people; their entire sense of self-esteem seemed bound up with whether or not they were ever going to make senior manager. They wouldn't date anybody further down the corporate food chain than them. Feeling unable to cope with my double workload of literature and IT, I headed to my local GP in East Dulwich, hoping perhaps to be prescribed anti-depressants or rest or both.

"I can't go on like this," I wailed.

"No, of course you can't", he glibly replied in a tone that implied that he didn't give a toss.

Part of me thinks it's unethical to encourage employees to sign out of EU working time regulations, since those rules were set in place to protect workers from exploitation. It's the ten grand joining bonus that lures them in. A likely looking piece of bait. *Chomp* – down comes the mouth upon the hook.

The decent manager, Ed, left for greener pastures and now works for J.K. Rolling-In-It. I had a nervous breakdown from the pressure, couldn't work out how to get home from work one day, was diagnosed with a brain tumour and now work for myself. Anybody who succeeds or stands out risks becoming a target. But I wonder about the other women. The ones who come along after me. No doubt they too will have been raised to believe that their hopes and dreams can be fulfilled. Then they end up with their heads in ovens.

Trickery, treachery, deception: if you read *Churchill's Wizards*, you'll begin to realize that the British admire these qualities. They are seen as valuable psychological tools – weapons to use against an enemy. Is that how they saw me – as an invader from the Antipodes, a foreign body?

Then there are the medical professionals. We are taught to put faith in them. To trust them. We don't expect to be harassed by a doctor, nor do we expect them to be negligent. If a man goes to the doctor he's taken seriously. A woman gets told "it's psychological". Even if she does have a genuine complaint – such as, for instance, a brain tumour.

My intuition and my perception were telling me not to continue in such a ruthless, cut-throat environment. I was too thin-skinned to be around these people all the time. I began hearing ominous music playing in my head each day as I was walking into work. I didn't want to end up like Amy Winehouse – a walking train wreck, with the onlookers gathered round, all feasting on the *Schadenfreude*. What good would fame do me anyway? You can't eat it. You can't sleep with it. Fame was fickle and capricious; here today, gone tomorrow. I found myself caught up in worlds that were glamorous, but treacherous. As slippery as black ice. You could easily go for a skate.

During my last days at work, I felt the borders of my world disintegrating; I was fading away, melting, like the Wicked Witch of the West. I started laughing and talking to myself.

Not fit to be in an office, read my last work assessment.

I was chain-smoking, down to forty-five kilos. A walking skeleton. I collapsed in the tube station, unable to find my way home from work and was admitted as an outpatient to the Maudsley. I was told that it was a psychiatric

107

emergency and that if I tried to go into work they would hospitalize me.

You are two feet away from complete psychological collapse, said the shrink. I laughed in his face. I couldn't help it. In times of extreme stress (being hit by a car, working seventy-hour weeks) I don't start crying, I laugh. Some people experience this phenomenon at funerals. They don't mean to be rude, or socially inappropriate; it's stress relief.

We've seen it all before, the nurses told me. *People work too hard, they get caught up in the rat race, they burn themselves out. They run out of energy.*

Don't go on your own, the Maudsley nurses told me when I suggested going to a Ware poets evening to meet Tamar Yoseloff and Co. I wonder why. Perhaps a woman on her own looks like prey to a predator. A man is allowed to be a lone wolf and nobody bothers him; a woman on her own is either socially retarded or just plain dumb or both.

Thank God for family. Dad flew over from New Zealand to help me get back on my feet. I had choices: I could stay in the UK or return to New Zealand. I made the decision to return to New Zealand, and I have to say I'm glad that I did. For three years or so I wondered if I really did have some sort of mental illness. At first I just accepted the doctor's diagnosis, which was burnout due to being in the grip of a manic episode. But something wasn't adding up. Why was I struggling to write a shopping list? Why couldn't I organize a ski trip?

The world is a dangerous place. Yet, why should I cower? Why should I hide away? Maybe it's a writer thing. Some of the best writers have been recluses. I've met my fair share of brain-boxes. They all seemed more confident than me, but maybe they were just faking it.

In my last days in London I was far from with it. I believe I may have had some kind of seizure, during which my spirit left my body. Where it went, nobody knows. Roaming in the Scottish highlands, perhaps, or malingering in the London Underground. A restless spirit; a hungry ghost with its sights set on reaching the other side. A dangerous high-wire act.

Three years and ten doctors later, they found the brain tumour in my left frontal lobe. They'd been all too eager to diagnose me as having manic depression, the mental illness du jour, but after sitting at home for three years, more bewildered and confused than manic or depressed, I knew that there must be something more wrong with me. They checked me into the local mental health unit, gave me an MRI and found a lump the size of a lemon. Millimeter by millimeter it invades my brain. It's not the death sentence I once thought it was; you can live for decades if you take them out. My neurosurgeon, Mr Mee, tells me that he operated on a couple of people with grade two astrocytomas in the 1980s and they're still going strong. Further, there could be bright spots on the horizon. Science advances all the time, and stem cell research is being pioneered. Perhaps in the future, somebody could grow a new piece of brain and implant it – which leaves me wondering how I would turn out if they did slot in a new brain segment. Would I emerge with a new personality? The tumour is in that area. Perhaps they could insert an extrovert segment so that I could cope with having a public persona. I could emerge a whole new woman. It'd make a good story.

Don't get me wrong: it wasn't all bad. There were cool parallels between the art world and the world of IT. Working for Fast Search and Transfer in Norway, I learnt that their CEO bought Ingmar Berman's estate. Nerds could be into art and film. Into music. Many developers get to listen to music all day on iTunes and nobody bothers them as long as they get the work done. It's not such a bad job, but to succeed in that world you probably have to be better at playing politics than I am, be far more cut-throat, more ruthless, more downright ambitious.

Sounds like a right shark pit, commented my father, when I reported back from the front line.

I think you're being a bit hard on yourself, said the Senior Executive I worked under.

But I didn't understand what he meant. *I* wasn't being hard on myself. *They* were being too hard on me. I didn't burst into tears. I simply *snapped*. I don't care now. Maybe I'm one of the lucky ones. I don't have to work in a sweat shop. I got the house. I'm in a safe place. I have support workers and parents who still care, despite the turbulent adolescent years. My honest feeling was that I was surrounded by corruption or that *all was phoney* as Bob Dylan says. Nobody was to be trusted. Everything was coated in sugar; enticing but bad for you. As for me – God, you'd think I were the devil.

DYING MATTERS

It's a strange thing, to watch somebody die, to contemplate the end of life. I was present when my grandmother passed away; to me, it seemed that she had what you would call 'a good death' - if there is such a thing. She came down with acute myeloid luekemia and was taken into North Shore hospital. The nurses kept putting needles into her to count her white blood cells. She was never alone. A scary thing, to die alone, with nobody to hold your hand. My mother's brother and his wife slept in the room with her one night, and then my father and mother would be in the room with her the next. The rest of her grandchildren were all present, saying their goodbyes in turn.

"It's just such a bugger, Laura", she said to me.

Earlier, she had said to my sister, "It's no fun, getting old, Nicola."

"The train is coming", she said, shortly before gasping her final breath. And then....gone. At least her spirit was. Her body lay lifeless, doll-like in the bed and my grandfather stood in the room with her, quietly, gently weeping. Her essence was elsewhere. Do I believe in life after death, in an afterlife? Have I got faith in a spirit realm or reincarnation? I recently had brain surgery to remove a tumor. The name of this beast is a bit of a tongue twister - oligodendroglioma. After the surgery I thought I could hear and see a DVD of my own funeral playing. I could hear my relatives speaking in turn. Spooky stuff. I'd had a small sub-acute haemmorage; dying must have been on my mind.

I'd like to believe I could come back as a cat, free to a good home, perhaps living with some little old lady who took good care of me.

"I've had a good life," said my grandmother, as she lay dying.

Could I say the same of my existence? It's certainly had its twists and turns, its ups and downs. Apparently, the tumor is genetic, not linked to smoking or drinking. I still feel guilty. I have abused my health and now I am paying the price, my body is saying 'enough's enough' and throwing up its hands in despair. Genetics and epigenetics. Surely there were external factors which contributed to the cancer. There's nothing I can do about it at this point. Too late now. Damage done. I belong to the local brain injury group. One man had a car fall on his head when the hoist, which was holding it up so he could examine underneath, snapped. He gets by, but there are times when he struggles to think. Blank spaces where thoughts should be.

What strikes me about brain injury is the randomness of it. How sudden and strange it is to be permanently injured in some brutal way. Strokes, haemmorages, vehicle accidents; these are just some of the injuries that have been inflicted on members of my brain injury group. We enjoy ourselves. We meet up for coffees and boat trips. Another guy had a large chunk of metal fly into his head when he was working down on the wharf. Now he's religious and wants me to join his prayer group. My mother's friend is praying for me too. And who's to say that prayers don't work? Maybe they do, the whispered words or thoughts spiraling upwards towards Heaven where God listens in with his right hand cupped around his ear.

How could anybody possibly claim that dying doesn't matter? How could the end of life ever be thought of as insignificant? Surely dying, inextricably intertwined with life as it is, is a major events. My father, who is right about many things, claims that after life there's just nothing. Imagine that; no eyesight, no hearing, no walking, no talking, no fighting, no loving. Nothing at all. It's hard to conceive of it. Does everything in life happen for a reason or is that just a platitude to make us feel better about events when life throws us a curve ball? How can a random whammy like a brain tumor fail to make a person depressed? Any major medical condition strikes a blow, makes us think about our own mortality. As Jarvis Cocker would say, 'We can't escape, we're born to die'. Born with a shelf life. And when it's over? Maybe when it's over that's it, kaput, final curtain.

One of the biggest lotteries in life is the family we are born into. You can choose your friends, but you can't choose your family, as they say. For better or for worse, you are stuck with them, unless, of course, you are one of those who ends up estranged from their whanau - even then they're still blood, thicker than water. What family doesn't have a rift in it? Discord and disharmony are as much a part of life as playing the right chords, living in harmony. They say you should never go to bed angry; I also believe that nor should a family member die with a rift in the family. Rifts exist to be healed. If somebody passes away you will never get the chance to forgive and forget, not properly. When disaster strikes it's a true test of character. How we bear up in the face of potential disaster says a lot about us as people. Do we fall to pieces or do we soldier on? Has anybody ever written about what it's like to die? I don't mean the onlookers, the people watching, but how is it to stand in the shoes of the person passing away? Oh yes, we've all heard about the Great White Light and moving towards it, but is that for real, or all just heresay? Hard to report back from the other side, unless you believe in spirits and ouija boards and all that jazz. Rapping out messages from the Great Beyond, with only the talented, the 'gifted' able to hear you and most of the rest of the world labelling them a sham or a kook. Maybe these notions of heaven, hell and purgatory are just inventions for we humans to placate ourselves with. To some people grief is a largely solitary affair, others grieve in groups. Maori people often wail at funerals, giving voice to their grief rather than repressing it; letting it all hang out. Hawaiin people practice kuwo - a form of vocal lamentation.

Death leaves a vacant space for the people left behind, the friends and family, each of whom grieves in their own way? They recover, they move on or, at least, they try to. Death can be quiet and expected, like my grandmother's, or sudden and violent, as in the case of a murder, a suicide, or plane crash. I was fourteen when my schoolmate Cindy Mosey's plane went down. She and some of her gymnastics club were flying to Wellington to take part in the national championships when the plane, flying low for sight-seeing purposes, hit a wire and went down. Cindy was the sole survivor. She got down in the space between seats, where your feet normally go and was spared death, was flung into the open ocean where she bobbed about for an hour or two before being picked up by the Cook Strait ferry and bundled to safety. The rest of the passengers and crew perished. A cliche I despise - whatever doesn't kill you makes you stronger. One of the reasons I don't favour this expression is that there are many people who don't become stronger through their experiences, but who are broken by them instead. People who lay down and die. However, maybe in Cindy's case it was true as she went on to become three times world kite surfing champion.

In 2015, our local MP is putting The End of Life Bill before parliament as a conscience vote. I pray it gets passed. What am I going to be like when my cancer hits grade 4, turns into the nasty glioblastoma multiforme, so named for its ability to take many different forms? The alternative name for glioblastoma multiforme is the terminator. Would you want something called The Terminator hanging out in your head? Will it cause me to lose bladder and/or bowel control? Will I be partially or totally paralysed, or lose my hearing and/or vision? How easy, how neat, to be able to dispense of myself with a simple tablet or injection, rather than pass through a lot of unnecessary and undignified suffering. Dignity, and the right to choose the manner and time of one's death is at the heart of the controversial End of Life debate. Surely it's better to give people the choice about how and when they go, rather than leaving it up to a callous god or cruel nature. Dying has never been pretty; it's one of the muckier sides of life. Life is full of struggle; the struggle to earn a living, the struggle to stay healthy, the fight to the death for the right to live your life. Should death be a struggle or more of a 'letting go'? And the tumor, can I learn to accept it, can I stop myself from asking 'is it real?' every fifteen minutes, thereby driving all the people around me crazy? Can I come to terms with the fact that other people sometimes refer to me as disabled?

The concept of death holds more questions than answers. How do I feel about leaving family behind? Will I make new friends or meet dead family on the other side? Then there is the question of timing. Will the man with the sickle arrive on cue,in approximately a decade, or will he wait a few more years, making me one of the long-term survivors? Both surgeons I consulted said the same thing 'I took these tumors out in the 80s and those people are still alive.' Undoubtably, they wanted to extend hope, but not false hope, they weren't lying, there really *are* long term survivors. There's still the option of chemotherapy should the tumor recur. The tumor has a special genetic co-deletion that predicts extended life and responsiveness to chemotherapy.

No fancy funeral for me; I'll be happy with a simple cremation. No fancy casket - just a cardboard box. Save costs.No elaborate ceremony either, I'll settle for a speech or two and maybe a song - Morrissey 'Sing Me To Sleep'. Why make a fuss? I was born,I lived, I died like gazillions of people before me. I hope that people read my books after I'm gone, but maybe that's just vanity. Maybe nobody will read a word and all my literary endeavours have been in vain.

With every centrimetre of brain I lose my life options begin to narrow. I still have choices. I went to an interview as a receptionist at a retirement home (back in the days when I still deluded myself that somebody would actually employ me.) I didn't get the job, but I loved the decor. I rang them; they're taking people with disabilities when they contract with the DHB in two weeks time. I fancy moving into one of their 'care apartments' - a kitchen/dining area, a bedroom and a bathroom, all brand new, just opened in 2013. You can smell the freshness. I had lunch there (free vouchers) and joined in with the book club afterwards. The sprightly ladies discussed what they had been reading and said they'd be glad to have some young blood in their midst. There'd be 24 hour nursing care available. If I sell my property that's where I'll be. Summerset in the Sun - doing lengths in the picturesque swimming pool, attempting to keep my cancer, my death, at bay.

THE TRANSCRIPTS OF VENUS

My lover Venus and I were sitting on our front porch, enjoying a gin and tonic and staring at the sky, when we saw a small speck moving across the face of the sun. I didn't think much of it at the time. However, later that evening, the two of us were watching the evening news when an article about the transit of Venus came on the television. There must have been some sort of problem with the reception. The voice of the announcer was barely discernible through the static.

The last transit was 243 years ago, in 1769, the same year that Captain Cook and his crew reached New Zealand. Theirs had been an epic journey. They had sailed around the world, discovered new races of humans and catalogued many thousands of different species. They had braved storms that had sprung up from nowhere and encountered strange creatures of the deep – giant squids, killer whales and great white sharks. Cook's mission had been to reach Tahiti before 1769 in order to build an astronomical observatory. England's Royal Academy, who were Cook's sponsors, hoped that he would be able to observe Venus gliding across the face of the sun and therefore measure the size of the solar system. Determining its size was one of the foremost problems confronting the eighteenth-century scientific community – an equivalent problem facing today's scientists is the nature of dark matter and dark energy. Unfortunately, the observations of the 1769 transit from 76 observatories around the globe, of which Cook's was one, weren't precise enough to determine the solar system's size. This feat wasn't achieved until the 19th century, when astronomers used photography to aid them.

Venus flicked off the TV with the remote.

"How exciting," she said. "We have witnessed a special event. A rarity."

I poured us another gin and we retired back to the porch.

#

The second, much larger speck didn't arrive until the following week. It was far more frightening than the first arrival. A luminous entity on the far horizon, it drew ever closer. It blocked out the sun. Birds fell from the sky; cattle in field next to the house started lowing.

Venus and I walked outside and watched the object descend.

"It's like *War of the Worlds*," hissed Venus.

The object drew closer, growing more ominous by the second.

Six spider-like legs descended. It came to land in the field next door to our house. It was eerily silent. Venus was terrified and ran inside, slamming the porch door shut behind her. I couldn't tear my eyes from the scene. A door was lowered from the side of the ship and two aliens strode down the gangplank, as bold as gold, bug eyes bulging from their bulbous heads. They made curious clacking noises. I expected some kind of greeting, something clichéd – *We come in peace,* or *Salutations, earthlings.* The silence seemed louder than sound.

I ran inside and grabbed a bottle of bubbly with which to greet our guests. As the first earthling to come face to face with these extra terrestrial visitors I wanted to make a good initial impression. I popped open the cork of the Veuve Cliquot and poured three glasses. It didn't occur to me that they might not like champers, or, more likely, not even know what it was. Nor did it cross my mind that it might not be part of their culture to greet arrivistes with drink. They didn't stop to sup, they walked straight past me. It was almost as if they didn't see me, as if I was invisible or perhaps didn't even exist at all. Venus had locked the front door, but the aliens were oblivious to the bolts. They charged inside, pushing down the door as if it was made of air. I followed them into the house. Somehow they seemed to know where the food was kept. They went straight to the fridge and began their raid. They must've been starving on their intergalactic flight, because they started stuffing their faces with smoked salmon, camembert cheese and quince paste. They made themselves at home. Flicked on the TV (which was still static-riddled), put up the footrest of the La-Z-Boy armchair, helped themselves to Venus's cigarettes and started smoking, not bothering with the ashtray, just casually flicking ash onto the floor. It was a strange invasion.

Even though they had been extremely rude to Venus and me, barging inside the house without asking, I still had to be polite back to them. If I pissed them off and they went postal and started killing off the country's inhabitants I'd be in deep trouble. Venus, a fiction writer by trade, had been working on a new novel for the gay porn market entitled *Sixty Shades of Gay*. One of the aliens spied the manuscript on the table and grabbed it. He opened up the black bag he carried with him and took out what appeared to be some sort of hand-held alien to English translation device. He must've bought it somewhere on Earth because it had a sticker reading *Babel* on the side. I doubt that the wider alien community would have been familiar with the Tower of Babel. He read the first page of the hand-written manuscript and started laughing hysterically, nudging his buddy. His friend grabbed a few pages of the script and cackled along. The first alien pushed the manuscript into his black bag and the two of them made for their spaceship having secured their bounty.

"Hey," shouted Venus. "That's my novel, my transcript!"

Unconcerned, the aliens sped up the gangplank and into the safety of the ship. The gangplank receded, the spaceship's motor revved and the ship disappeared into the inky vastness of the solar system.

Venus slumped back onto the couch.

"Oh God," she moaned. "All my hard work and talent. Eight months I've been working on that novel and now it's gone. I knew I should've used my P.C., but there's just something about ink."

Venus had always insisted on writing her books in longhand with her grandmother's fountain pen.

"Never mind," I said. "*Sixty Shades of Gay* is sure to be a hit amongst the gay alien community."

"Oh great. My agent probably could have sold my masterpiece for a six-figure sum and instead it'll be used to entertain aliens. Good to know that somebody's having a laugh."

She took a cigarette from her pack and lit up.

"You'll be famous throughout the solar system," I said. "Who cares about Planet Earth? We're just a tiny blip. Keep the bigger picture in mind. Conquering outer space is far more important than our puny old third rock from the sun."

Nobody but us two had seen the ship descend – our hick town was in the middle of nowhere, and our nearest neighbour was three miles away from our cattle ranch. There would've been mass hysteria if pictures of the alien craft had been released onto the internet and to the media. Venus wasn't much consoled by the fact that she may have had a hit in the alien gay community. She sank into a deep depression from which she refused to budge. She lay in bed for three weeks, lamenting the loss of her precious manuscript.

During her convalescence, I tended to the cattle alone, feeding them bales of hay, shifting them from paddock to paddock when they had consumed all the grass in their current enclosure. At night I cooked meals for Venus and took them in to her. She ate them sitting upright in bed.

When the three weeks was up she emerged from her cocoon. She showered, dressed and prepared herself to re-write the entire novel from scratch, this time giving a name to her formerly nameless hero – Clifford Forsyth.

#

NOTE: The following transcript has been translated from the Alverian.

He'd carried it off. He'd secured for himself the most precious possession in the entire universe.
With the valuable goods tucked safely under one arm and a megaphone in hand, Zador strode purposefully into the crowded bazaar, fully prepared to hustle.
"What fools," he cackled. "Such a precious item to be so insufficiently guarded. I must secure the best possible deal."

Already a small crowd was gathering. Somebody tried to steal the manuscript from under Zador's arm, but he snatched it away. It would not be stolen. It would be sold for a hefty sum, enough to keep him fed, clothed and watered for the rest of his life. He needed to generate interest, an air of excitement. A feeling that he had in his possession an item of value that would not be selling cheap. He raised the megaphone to his lips.

"For sale to the highest bidder. A genuine 100% authentic super-duper quality earth manuscript, freshly *err*...acquired."

Three fellow Alverians gathered around him along with a Brigian or two, nostrils quivering with excitement.

"I'd like to look at it," said a young female Alverian.

"Only from a distance," said Zador.

He didn't want anybody's grubby fingers smudging the ink.

"Could you tell us a little bit about the plot?"

"Gay sex, gay sex and more gay sex," said Zador, who had scribbled out Venus's name and written his own on the cover. "Sure to be a hit throughout the solar system and possibly also on an extra-solar scale. Couldn't have been written on this planet. It's really out of this world."

Already, his mind spun with the thought of all the money that could be generated from merchandising. Gay porn action figures, posters, coffee cups – the works.

A rather aloof-looking alien stood apart from the rest: Xorian, managing director of Uni-Solar Books, one of the most powerful publishing houses in the solar system. He wore a pinstriped grey suit teamed with a ruffled red shirt and paisley cravat. One dwarf alien stood either side of him. He did not approach Zador himself. Instead, he sent one of his minions to speak with him. He offered a hefty sum for the manuscript, and Zador snapped it up, holding out his wrist, microchip-side up, so Xorian could zap his cash card over it. The manuscript was his.

Once word got round Alveria that a precious piece of gay porn was about to be released onto the market, the government came down heavy. They were an oppressive bunch – staunch anti-homosexuals. They jailed anybody displaying homosexual tendencies. *Sixty Shades of Gay* was banned throughout the solar system, but the Gay Alien Liberation Front had been gathering force for some time. This cherished manuscript was booty in their war against oppression. The government could stop the manuscript from being released onto bookshelves, but they couldn't prevent it from hitting the solar-web, where it would spark a revolution. Gay Alverian Pride. Homosexual aliens, who had once been forced to cower indoors, could walk boldly down the street, shoulders back, heads held high, fluffy pink feather boas wrapped around their necks.

One of Xorian's minions typed up the novel and made it available for download. It was a huge hit amongst the gay alien community who related to the frankness with which the book was written. Zador's life was forever changed. He couldn't walk down the street without being mobbed by screaming fans. At first he enjoyed the attention, but after six months of complete strangers banging at his door and begging for an introduction, he longed for nothing more than to be left in peace, to be anonymous. They hounded him with questions. *How long had it taken him to write the novel? Was any of it based on fact, or was it all completely fictitious? Were there to be any sequels?*

The fans weren't satisfied with just the book. They wanted a piece of Zador, they wanted to touch him, to maul him. They wanted more words, sequels. Zador, who, to be perfectly frank, had only read the first third of the novel anyway, was unsure about how to solve the problem of producing more work. It was his father, Tritan, who suggested he revisit earth in order to capture for himself the woman who had produced the first tour de force.

Zador descended to Earth in the dead of night. Silver-tongued though he was, he knew that he wouldn't be able to persuade Venus to go with him of her own volition. He peered in through the living room window, pressed his nose up to the pane, his large eyes prominent in his forehead. She was sitting up at the dining table, reading. He could even see the title of the novel – *To The Lighthouse.* Her laptop sat in front of her on the table. The other biped, whom he assumed to be her partner, was nowhere in sight. Zador smashed the glass pane with his fists, which were steel plated, like those of all Alverians. Venus screamed as Zador climbed over the sill and then picked his way across the glass fragments. He gagged her with one hand and dragged her out through the front door to where the motor of his spaceship revved.

Once they landed on Alveria, Zador took Venus into his house and fastened a chain around her ankle. The other end was secured into the wall. Using his translation device, he explained his modus operandi to her. She was big throughout the solar system, he said – even if it was his name on the novel's cover. He would be the front end of the operation and she would be the back end. When he said this to her, she imagined one of those pantomime

cows – with one person in the rear end of the costume and another in the front. He was dependent on her literary brain, he said. Food here came in the form of a small orange-coloured pill. That's why Zador and friend had hoed into the earth food so greedily. Real food was not unknown on Alveria, but it was a scarcity and therefore available only at special ceremonies such as the Queen's birthday (the Alverians didn't call her a queen, of course, they called her a Rocadam, but she had the same functions as an earthly monarch such as Queen Elizabeth.)
You will be allowed out for two hours of exercise per day, conveyed Zador via his Babel translator.

Venus had mixed thoughts about being Zador's literary slave. She had struggled for years to get a manuscript accepted for publication on Earth. Now, according to Zador, she was big throughout the solar system, on most of the planets apart from Earth. For her, writing had always been about reaching readers, rather than becoming wealthy or famous. So, at least she had achieved that goal. On the other hand, why should Zador get to put *his* name to *her* work? *She* was the one with the talent, *she* was the one who'd done all the hard work – why should Zador take all the credit? Still, that's how it was for now. She'd just have to accept it.

Venus had seen some of the planet as they had descended from the skies. There was no grass, but rather a sort of light pink astro-turf that covered the ground. There were multi-coloured trees and odd-looking animals with long fur that had wheels instead of feet. She learned from Zador that they were called Pinooks. The air was warm and smelt faintly of jasmine. Alveria had three suns and so the climate was hot and dry. Most of the aliens wore burka-style garments, so as not to get too burnt. It might not be the sort of world she would choose for herself, but she could probably get used to it. At any rate – she didn't see that she had any choice. She wasn't too sure what the Alverians did for entertainment – apart from reading gay porn. Gravity here was heavier than on earth. When Zador took her out for walks, Venus's limbs felt as heavy as lead.

Although Zador tried to keep it a secret that the true author of the treasured gay porn had landed on their planet, word soon got out, having been leaked by one of Zador's many servants. Fairly soon, Zador's bungalow was surrounded by fans eager to catch a glimpse of the author. Zador was forced to tape black paper to the windows in order to secure their privacy. Venus was hard at work on her sequel to *Sixty Shades of Gay – Sixty Shades Gayer.* When Zador took her out for their evening stroll – with Venus on a harness – she was stared at by the locals. Nobody can stare like an alien.

Zador's father, Tritan, took an instant liking to Venus and treated her like a second daughter. He understood that she might be suffering culture shock, and he slipped her tidbits of information that might help her get along in her new environment.

"Always keep your burka on when you go outdoors. Not only will our three suns fry you if you remove your outer garment, but the alien men will lose their minds at the sight of bare human flesh. You should try and get along with Zador. I know he's holding you captive, but he's not such a bad sort underneath it all. It's just that he doesn't have any marketable skills himself and so he had to find somebody else to…exploit."

From day one, Venus began to plot her escape. She didn't intend to be Zador's word slave, stuck in his sweatshop forever. She decided to write *Sixty Shades Gayer* as badly as possible so that Zador would let her be released. *Sixty Shades of Gay* had been targeted at gay men – the sequel would target gay women.

Katie licked the last remnants of whipped cream from around Monica's nipples, wrote Venus.
Patricia smoothed coconut butter over Henrietta's rotund buttocks.

Sixty Shades Gayer was released via the solar-web and was even more successful than *Sixty Shades of Gay*, selling over 10 million copies. The lesbian aliens were lapping it up. Parades were organized; proud female aliens dressed up in purple strutted down the street. It was a revolution. Hordes of screaming gays were to be found lined up outside Zador's house. They smashed the window panes; they tore away the black paper. They forced their way inside. Venus was terrified. They weren't satisfied with the manuscript; they wanted a piece of her. The fans bombarded her with questions, just as they had done to Zador. *Is the novel autobiographical? How long did it take to write? Where had she got the main plot idea from?* they asked. Venus had felt like replying *What plot idea?* but she didn't speak the words. The novel was just lesbian sex from start to finish. The Rocadam was even reported to have a copy of the feted manuscript in her possession. At first Venus had thought that this was just hearsay, but then the Rocadam invited Venus to her castle in order to have her read to her. Venus thought twice about accepting the invitation. She was a little intimidated. She was a writer, a recluse, she wasn't used to dining with queens. However, the Rocadam had a reputation for barbequing alive those who refused to do her bidding, so she thought she had better obey. Zador set her free for the evening. He, too, did not dare disobey the monarch.

The palace sat atop a high hill near Alveria's South Pole. It was a foreboding building and Venus trembled a little as she approached its moat. In her hands she clutched tight the invitation she had received.

Dear Venus,

Please accept an invitation to dine at Hilltop Castle Saturday 22nd December 2012

Little was known about the Rocadam's private life. Nobody knew whether or not she had a partner. Nobody knew if she'd had any education (although probably she'd had a series of tutors as a girl). As Venus crossed the bridge to enter the castle, the alligators in the moat beneath her feet snapped their jaws at her. She drew her maroon velvet cloak more tightly about her person, as if fighting off a cold wind.

The doors to the palace were made of material similar to oak and were two metres high. Venus gathered her courage and knocked to announce her arrival. The doors swung open and the valet greeted her. He escorted her down the hallway and into a large dining room set with crystal and fine china, then pulled out a chair. Venus sat down and the valet exited the room, leaving her alone for a good five minutes. Finally, a woman whom Venus assumed was the Rocadam entered. She walked with an air of authority. By Christ, she was ugly! There was a gigantic wart, with a number of large hairs sprouting out of it, positioned at the base of her nose. Her forehead protruded from her face, even more prominently than in a typical alien. Her ears were enormous and she walked with a lolloping gait. She was obese; her stomach hung out over the top of her jeans. She, too, carried a Babel translator.

"Hello, I am Moreda, the Rocadam."

Her translated words came worming up out of the machine.

"N-n-nice to meet you," replied Venus.

The Rocadam sat down at the other end of the enormous dining table. A roast goose, surrounded with potatoes, was brought out on a silver platter, along with two bowls of steaming green vegetables. The two of them dined in an awkward silence, which was broken only by the clacking of cutlery on china. When the meal was finished, Moreda bought forth her copy of *Sixty Shades Gayer* for Venus to sign. Venus signed. The Rocadam tapped the pen against the page and indicated that Venus should place a lipstick kiss upon its inside front cover. Venus didn't dare to disobey. God only knew what lesbian fantasies were flitting through the monarch's mind as she looked at her. The Rocadam walked her back to the edge of the moat and bade her goodnight.

These dinners with the Rocadam became a monthly, then a fortnightly and then a weekly occurrence. Venus started work on *Sixty Shades Gayest*. This new friendship with Moreda was putting the lead back in her pencil, the ink back in her pen. The new novel was flowing from her fingertips as if it was being dictated from on high. Venus did something she'd never done before; she shared drafts with another person – Moreda. She expected Moreda to slam her efforts, but instead she was gently encouraging. She egged Venus on when she was flagging. Gave her bunches of tulips to take home after the dinners. Venus did not care that Moreda was ugly. She had lovely manners and a winning smile. When Moreda smiled the ice around Venus' heart melted. And, although she hated to admit that her heart had been won this way, Moreda was a way for Venus to get real food, rather than just subsisting on the orange pills. Moreda was grateful to Venus for liberating her, for allowing her to come out of the closet. She hadn't openly admitted her sexuality to herself until *Sixty Shades of Gay* had hit the alien market.

Venus had been dining with Moreda for six months when she popped the question. Filled the dining room with roses. Went down on one knee and proposed. Venus knew that Zador would be consumed with jealousy. She suspected, although of course Zador would not admit it, that he had a crush on her. All the little signs were there. If she was late home from Moreda's he would start questioning her. *Why are you late? What has Moreda been talking to you about?*
Why did he care…unless? If it boiled down to a choice between the two aliens, she would choose Moreda. Zador just treated her like a slave, an object to make him rich. Moreda treated her properly, like a queen, which is indeed what she would become if they married. Two queens reigning happily over their subjects.

The happy day was set for the following spring. Xorian hadn't been too worried when he first heard that his precious tomes weren't being written by Zador, but by an earthling called Venus. As long as the material kept getting produced he was happy. However, now that Venus was to marry Moreda, thus freeing herself from Zador's grasp, how would his cash cow keep producing milk? Not a man given to panic, he sent one of his minions around to visit Venus in order to negotiate working directly with her on the sequels and cutting out Zador. Venus was more than happy with this arrangement. Zador was miffed, but powerless. Venus delivered the final novel in the trilogy, *Sixty Shades Gayest*, to one of Xorian's dwarves. *Sixty Shades Gayest* featured gay aliens and was packed with insights into the alien psyche.

The grand day dawned. The trees were in bloom, bursting forth with blossom. Venus didn't have any friends amongst the aliens, just fans, many of whom turned up for the wedding. The wedding day was also the launch of the third in the trilogy of novels – *Sixty Shades Gayest*. Gigantic cardboard covers were displayed at random around the palace. The wedding was beamed around the universe via satellite, watched by millions of alien viewers; all those who had not been fortunate enough to be invited to the wedding.

Venus was glad that she finally had a chance to meet and talk with some aliens other than Moreda and Zador. An Alverian wedding is a strange affair. Most of the aliens were salivating at the thought of real food as they crossed the moat. A number of Pinooks had been recruited as waiters. They moved around the room, the wheels that supported them creaking as they did so.

There was a gigantic cake in the shape of a spaceship – complete with flashing lights. There were several different types of meat and plenty of roast potatoes and vegetables for all. Zador received an invitation to the wedding. Nobody on the planet dared to refuse an invitation from the Rocadam. Moreda was too butch to wear a crown to the wedding, but she'd had one especially fashioned for Venus – it was hot pink with jewels set into it. Moreda wore a sombre black suit, but Venus was dressed in shiny gold satin with a prominent silver sash.

Because real food was such a valued commodity in Alveria, at the end of the wedding the guests began to throw food at Venus, in a parody of the Cypriot custom of pinning money to the bride. The wedding ended with a special highlight, which Venus and Moreda had been planning for months. The two lesbians beckoned to Zador. He followed them across the moat and towards a nearby hill. Scantily clad female aliens were lined up either side of the path. They were foot soldiers – not important enough to have been invited to the event. They beat drums in time. In defiance of Alveria's three suns, they wore ragged leather dresses, which were slanted over one shoulder with a single strap. The dresses only just covered the buttocks and they had a row of tassels around the hem. Suddenly, Moreda lunged at Zador, pushing him to the ground. She tied his hands and his feet and put a gag into his mouth to muffle his high-pitched screams.

High atop the hill sat an alien made of wicker. Queen Moreda hoisted Zador up onto her right shoulder in a fireman's carry, and walked with him up the steps and into the wicker man. She deposited him on the floor of the effigy. The effigy was set alight and the women cackled and cheered as Zador burned. The novels were re-released under Venus's name. They were downloaded onto e-readers throughout the solar system and were a surprise hit back on Planet Earth.

The two women were kind monarchs – a gay Kate and Wills of the alien world. They enjoyed ruling over Planet Alveria. The aliens, in turn, treated them properly, even though Venus wasn't one of them. Because the two rulers were not oppressive, there was no uprising, no backlash. Unable to produce children of their own, Venus and Moreda adopted two young twin female aliens who were the result of an unwanted pregnancy. Alien sex was a strange affair, with the relevant organs being located in the middle of the back. Aliens, once born, were carried around in a marsupial-style pouch located in the front centre of the body. The adopted children were born premature and underweight, but Venus fed them real food and they soon grew strong and healthy. Their names were Juna and Leka and following the deaths of their adoptive parents they ascended to the throne and reigned in glory. In time they read to their own children from Venus's books, making appropriate adjustments for age as they went, and later they read to their children's children too.

GUEST POST: LAURA SOLOMON - THE LONG WALK HOME

Do authors dream of electric books? Yes, they most certainly do. At least in this day and age, where the e-book has the potential to revolutionise the literary industry. For me the e-book signifies power to the people. A small-timer like me can write their e-book and make it available for all the world to download – either by using a publisher or by doing it themselves.

The problem then becomes, not how do I get an agent or publisher, but how do I attract readers? How do I compete with the other five million books on Amazon and Kobo? I don't claim to have the answer to this question. Social media can help with promotion. Online reviews as well as reviews in traditional media such as newspapers, magazines, radio and television all contribute as do word of mouth and literary prizes.

When I view the statistics for my website, I see that the vast majority of the people who have come to the site have found me via Facebook. I'm not into Twitter and I don't use Facebook to convey details of my every action, as glamorous and exciting as that would be (*Woke up, ate breakfast, sat at laptop. Walked to beach. Walked home from beach. Ate lunch. Sat at laptop. Ate dinner. Slept. Repeat ad infinitum.*) I do, however, use Facebook to create online book launches, complete with virtual canapés and champers. For me, Facebook and e-books are a way to cut through some of the snobbery that has traditionally been prevalent in the industry. It also speeds things up a lot. No longer do I have to submit a manuscript and wait and wait and *wait* for an acceptance. Via

Facebook I have managed to befriend over two thousand people, most of them writers. Chances are there's an inverse relationship between Facebook friends and real ones. But, even better, at least four of those writers have been invaluably helpful to me, and I, in turn, have tried to be helpful to them. Ola Rhodes and I swap stories via Facebook and provide comments and advice on each other's work. Murray Alfredson, in Australia, is currently reading my novel, *An Imitation of Life*, about an insect-eating giantess and providing valuable editorial tips in time for the release of the second edition. Jan Needle, in the UK, has a new imprint *Skinback Books*, to which I intend to submit a novella I am currently working on. These new relationships would never have occurred if it were not for the advent of Facebook. And, via good old Facebook, I have re-met Catherine Chidgey, whom I originally met at a writer's conference in 1998 and she has agreed to work with me on the second edition of my novel, *Hilary and David*. Some authors love the limelight, but for a Janet Frame-style troglodyte like me who loathes being lured out of her bat-cave, the e-book/Facebook combo suits me down to the ground.

It's shark on shark action as writers compete for readers. I'm not sure what the success of *Fifty Shades of Grey* tells us about today's society. That there are a lot of sexually unsatisfied women who are turning to Mummy porn to fulfill their needs? Maybe today's women are so busy juggling career, family and all the other demands made of them that all they want at the end of a hard day is to come home from work, sink into a hot lavender-scented bath and lose themselves in a good porno. Maybe it's women's revenge. Porn has traditionally been made for and consumed by men. Maybe the tide, the tables, are turning. Women, too, are claiming their right to be titillated.

Myself, I would squirm if I had to write soft porn. I'm a nice middle-class girl, with two and a half degrees who writes what I suppose you would call 'literary fiction', although I am against such classifications myself. For me the rise of the e-book is extremely liberating. If I fall out with a publisher, it's not so disastrous. I can always upload the book to Amazon and Kobo myself, or partner with somebody running an e-book imprint. Don't get me wrong. I don't make any money doing all of this. My last royalties cheque came in at the grand sum of twenty quid. I put it towards my new Ferrari. The one I'll buy when my next royalties cheque (for forty quid) comes through the post. So, why do I continue? I don't have the answer to that question either. I've been writing fiction since my teens. Like most writers, I've also worked either full or part-time for a lot of my life to support myself. I'm so full of ideas, you could wire me up like one of P.K.Dick's precogs and make movies out of my thought-dreams. In fact, I'm sure somebody would have done so by now, if they thought they could make money out of it. And if they thought they could get away with it, without having Amnesty International beating down the door. In fact, I make so little money, that I might as well give the damned books away for free.

Then we have the rise of the blog. I myself am the December guest blogger, so I will try and impart some useful advice to all you wanna-be writers out there. *Don't bother. Do you really want to be a thirty-eight year old loser like me, stuck at home all day, churning out crap that nobody wants to read, let alone pay for?* Exactly. Enjoy your life, keep your day job, find a girl (or boy), settle down, have kids, raise a family, mow the lawn, go see a film, go jogging, do anything except write fiction.

Because it seems to me that in this day and age, unless you can break into the Mummy porn market, you're *doomed.*